Flint had to think of his son.

His desire to keep Lana at a distance tried to raise its head, but his gratitude about Logan's safety put his own concerns into perspective.

Logan took priority. And if Lana would agree to be Logan's nanny on a temporary basis, that would be best for Logan. And Flint would tolerate her nearness. Somehow.

"Can she, Daddy?" Logan asked, his face eager.

He turned to Lana. "Can you?" he asked her.

Lana drew in a breath and studied them both, and Flint could almost see the wheels turning in her brain.

He could see mixed feelings on her face, too. Fondness for Logan. Mistrust of Flint himself.

Maybe a little bit of… What was that hint of pain that wrinkled her forehead and darkened her eyes?

Finally, Lana gave a definitive nod. "All right," she said. "We can try it. I'll be your nanny, Logan."

* * *

Lone Star Cowboy League: Boys Ranch
Bighearted ranchers in small-town Texas

The Rancher's Texas Match by Brenda Minton
October 2016

The Ranger's Texas Proposal by Jessica Keller
November 2016

The Nanny's Texas Christmas by Lee Tobin McClain
December 2016

The Cowboy's Texas Family by Margaret Daley
January 2017

The Doctor's Texas Baby by Deb Kastner
February 2017

The Rancher's Texas Twins by Allie Pleiter
March 2017

Lee Tobin McClain read *Gone with the Wind* in the third grade and has been a hopeless romantic ever since. When she's not writing angst-filled love stories with happy endings, she's getting inspiration from her church singles group, her gymnastics-obsessed teenage daughter and her rescue dog and cat. In her day job, Lee gets to encourage aspiring romance writers in Seton Hill University's low-residency MFA program. Visit her at leetobinmcclain.com.

Books by Lee Tobin McClain

Love Inspired

Lone Star Cowboy League: Boys Ranch

The Nanny's Texas Christmas

Rescue River

Engaged to the Single Mom
His Secret Child
Small-Town Nanny

The Nanny's
Texas Christmas

Lee Tobin McClain

⊕ **HARLEQUIN**® LOVE INSPIRED®

Special thanks and acknowledgment
are given to Lee Tobin McClain for her contribution to the
Lone Star Cowboy League: Boys Ranch miniseries.

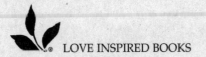

LOVE INSPIRED BOOKS

Recycling programs
for this product may
not exist in your area.

ISBN-13: 978-0-373-04474-0

The Nanny's Texas Christmas

Copyright © 2016 by Harlequin Books S.A.

www.Harlequin.com

Printed in U.S.A.

Now unto Him that is able to do exceeding abundantly above all that we ask or think, according to the power that worketh in us, unto Him be glory in the church by Christ Jesus throughout all ages, world without end.
—*Ephesians* 3:20–21

To my coworker Judith Reyna,
who always makes time to answer my silly
Spanish questions; and to my farmer friend Ben,
who helped me understand ranch equipment
and ranch foreman duties. And to Shana Asaro
and the amazing writers who worked together
on the Lone Star Cowboy League: Boys Ranch
books—Margaret Daley, Deb Kastner,
Jessica Keller, Brenda Minton and Allie Pleiter.
It's been a pleasure writing with you!

Chapter One

"Not again." Flint Rawlings frowned as he clicked up the volume on his cell phone and backed into the barn. He motioned to the three teenagers in front of him to keep working on the hay swather that lay disassembled in the dirt parking area.

"I'm terribly sorry." Mrs. Toler, his son's elderly nanny, sounded upset. "I've looked all around the cabin and yard. I suspect he's run off with that gang of hooligans from the ranch."

"He won't have gotten far. I'm sure he's up at the main house, just like last time." At six, Logan had developed a habit of running away, but he always went to the same place. "Don't you get yourself stressed out, Mrs. Toler. I'll go right over there and find him."

"All right, but, Flint…" Mrs. Toler paused, then spoke again, her voice shaky. "This just isn't going to work."

"What's that?" He pinched the bridge of his nose as the rising sound of a teen argument came through the barn's open doors.

"He's picking up some of the same bad habits that brought those delinquent boys to the ranch. Why, you wouldn't believe how he mouthed off when I told him he couldn't have a second piece of cake."

"The mouthing off will stop. I'll talk to him."

"Please, do. But meanwhile, I'm too old to be running all over the Triple C looking for that boy. I'm giving notice."

Flint restrained the groan that wanted to emerge from deep in his chest. "You go home and get some rest, and we'll talk later tonight." More like he'd beg her to stay on.

"Don't worry about Logan. I'll find him. I always do."

The stack of overdue paperwork he'd hoped to tackle this afternoon seemed to glare at him, but he turned away and headed outside. The teenagers were arguing over what engine part went where. Flint put a stop to that and explained to the boys that they'd have to take up their large-equipment-repair lesson tomorrow after school.

Then he headed up to the main house double time. He'd spoken reassuringly to Mrs. Toler, but the reality was that Logan was just six. Although the two of them had moved to their little cabin on the Triple C Ranch over a month ago, Logan didn't know the Triple C nearly as well as he'd known the Silver Star, the previous location of the Lone Star Cowboy League's Boys Ranch.

What if Logan had gotten lost? The days were at their shortest in early December, and the weather was getting steadily cooler.

Logan was notorious for forgetting to grab a jacket before running outside.

And Flint, rushed as he'd been with the move and the general craziness of a working ranch for at-risk boys, didn't always think to remind him.

A familiar sense of inadequacy rose in him. He'd been doing his best to raise Logan alone, but he wasn't one of those cookie-baking, playgroup-organizing kind of fathers featured in the parenting magazines he dutifully subscribed to. He was a ranch foreman, a veteran, a man's man. Which worked great with older boys, but as the single dad of a six-year-old, he wasn't passing muster.

Two of the teenagers he'd been working with raced ahead toward the main ranch house. Automatically he turned to see whether the third boy was coming, the one who'd looked the most disappointed when Flint had postponed the lesson. Robby Gonzalez was a new resident at the ranch, thirteen but big for his age, and he was kicking at a stone as he walked along behind.

Flint felt a twist of sympathy despite his own troubles. "C'mere, Robby." He gestured for the boy to join him. "Need some help."

Robby brightened and jogged to catch him. "*¿Qué pasa?* I mean, what's up?"

Flint considered trying to answer the kid in Spanish and decided against it. He knew a little, like most folks in this part of Texas, but he was too worried to find the right words. "Know where the younger kids are hanging out?"

"*Sí.* Most of them were going to the library. They said Senorita Alvarez was doing story time."

Miss Alvarez. Logan's pretty teacher, who volunteered at the ranch after school. Flint's certainty about where Logan had gone bumped up a notch, along with his discomfort.

"I saw Senorita Alvarez," Robby continued

with a sly grin. "She could read me a story anytime. *Es muy atractiva!*"

"Respect, Robby," Flint said automatically. The boy was probably too young to be interested in girls his own age, or at least, too awkward to know how to interact with them. But a crush on an older teacher? Maybe. Or maybe the kid was just trying to get attention—something all the at-risk boys craved. Flint thumped Robby's shoulder. "You did a good job helping to take apart that swather," he told the young teenager. "Make sure you show up tomorrow, and we'll put it back together."

Robby beamed and turned toward the main ranch house, and Flint veered off toward the little library behind it. He wished he could put his life back together as easily as a broken piece of farm equipment.

Mrs. Toler, their third babysitter this year, had seemed like a perfect solution to Flint's child-care problems. But Flint should have known it wouldn't work for long. The Lord didn't tend to look out for Flint and Logan. Never had.

Consciously relaxing his fists, Flint strode toward the library. Once inside the doorway, he stopped dead.

Amid a small group of the ranch's youngest residents, Logan was cuddled up on a low couch right beside his slender, long-legged teacher. His towhead shone bright against her dark, wavy hair.

The sight hurt. It was what he'd imagined he'd see with Logan's mother, until Stacie had decided she was too young to be tied down and dumped them both. As he'd scrambled to learn to care for his baby son alone, he'd vowed he wouldn't let a woman get close again, lest she break Logan's heart.

Never mind his own heart. After six years, it had pretty much frozen over.

Which didn't explain why he felt compelled to stand, watching, just one more minute. Watching his son laugh and cuddle in a carefree way, looking happier than he had in weeks. Just one more minute before he went and tore Logan away from the things he wanted most in the whole world: a big family of boys, and a whole lot of warm mothering.

Flint forced down his emotions. Logan *wasn't* one of the ranch's troubled residents. Whatever Flint's failings as a father, he'd provided his son with a safe home and good discipline. Flint didn't mind Logan's befriending the residents—after all, they all rode the same bus to the local public school and played together on the playground—but from what Mrs. Toler had said, Logan was picking up some bad habits. And while Flint didn't consider the young residents hooligans and delinquents, as Mrs. Toler did, he had to acknowledge that Logan might have learned some inappropriate language and attitudes.

Which had to stop.

Not only that, but Logan was distracting Lana Alvarez from the boys clustered around her feet, the ones she'd come to work with.

He was taking attention from kids who truly needed her help.

And in the process, Logan was getting way too attached to his teacher. No more. Flint needed to get his son out of there.

He'd just take one more minute to watch Logan looking so happy.

Lana Alvarez's heart went out to the little boy who kept pressing closer and closer to her side. Funny, Logan Rawlings *wasn't* one of the at-risk residents, but he seemed just as needy as they were. She wondered if his single dad even knew where he was.

"Scoot in closer," she said to the five other first-and second-grade boys clustered around her, patting the couch on her other side to encourage shy little Timmy Landon to sit there. He slid in, hesitantly, and Lana smiled at him.

No question, she adored kids. All of them. And even though she probably wouldn't have any of her own—not now, not after her single humiliating attempt at a normal relationship—she was blessed to be able to love so many kids through her day job as a teacher and through her volunteer work.

She turned the page of the illustrated book they were reading together and held it so all the boys could see the picture. "What do you think's going to happen next?"

"I know!"

"Me, me!"

"Uh-oh." Beside her, Logan tensed, looking toward the door.

Through which a very big, very handsome, very displeased-looking cowboy was coming their way.

Flint Rawlings. That curious flush she felt every time she saw him came on strong. It was probably annoyance, because he had to be the most aloof, inattentive father on the planet.

At least from what she'd seen. She knew she shouldn't judge, but when a child's best interests were at stake, it was hard for her to help it.

She put a protective arm around Logan, who'd pressed even closer as his father reached their little group.

"My son's not supposed to be here." His voice sounded accusatory, and she felt Logan cringe.

Men. If it weren't for that fact that she needed to model politeness to these young boys, she'd chew out the cowboy for his sharp tone and the way he was speaking to her instead of his son.

"Nice to see you." She allowed the slightest hint of censure to show in her voice as she extended her hand.

His face reddened. He reached out and wrapped his hand around hers. "Likewise."

The gravelly voice and the feel of his work-hardened hand raised her heart rate, and she pulled away, feeling suddenly flustered. What was *that* all about?

"Come on, Logan," Flint said, squatting

down. "You've worried Mrs. Toler so much that she had to go home. You'll have to come back to work with me."

Logan drew closer to Lana, his lower lip thrusting out. "I want to hear the rest of the story."

"Logan." The word was stern, sharp.

Too stern and sharp for a little boy, in Lana's opinion. But, she reminded herself, everyone had a different style of parenting.

On the other hand, this was working into a family fight that the rest of the boys didn't need to see. "He's welcome to stay with me," she offered. "I'm here until five. I'll be tutoring some of the kids after story time, and I'm sure Logan would be no trouble."

"Please, Daddy?"

Flint's eyes narrowed, and a shadow crossed his face. "No. I want him to come with me." He reached down, effortlessly picked Logan up, and set him on his feet outside the group.

Two big tears rolled down Logan's face despite his obvious attempt not to cry, and Lana's heart broke a little. She opened her mouth to protest, but a look from Flint quelled her.

Of course, a parent had more say over a child's life than a teacher. She had to remember she was just a teacher.

Would always be just a teacher.

"Thank you for looking out for him," Flint said stiffly. Then he took Logan's hand, and they walked away, the small boy straightening his back and trying to match his cowboy-booted steps to his father's longer strides.

Lana's throat felt tight. She beckoned for one of the boys to hand her the water bottle she always carried, took a long drink, and then forced a smile onto her face. "Okay, boys. Where were we?"

Two days later, Flint walked into the tack room to get out some saddles for the younger boys' evening riding lesson. His two-year-old black Lab, Cowboy, trotted along beside him.

Only, the saddles weren't there.

He looked around, wondering if one of the riding instructors had moved them, and then walked out into the main barn. Five minutes of searching didn't turn them up.

That left one likely culprit. "Logan!"

Since Mrs. Toler had definitely quit, he'd had Logan around the barn after school, which had meant some extra trouble and mischief. But last night, Flint had called around, and the result was a friend for Logan to play with today. A friend from school, not the ranch.

Flint liked the kids here at the ranch, knew that most were decent boys who'd gotten in trouble due to home problems that weren't their fault. But he didn't want them to be Logan's only friends. Martin Delgado was the son of a local doctor and, according to Logan, the smartest boy in the class.

What he should have asked Logan, Flint realized now, was how often the boy got in trouble.

Logan's blond head peeked in the barn door and was immediately joined by a dark one. Both faces looked guilty.

Flint restrained a smile. "Did you take the saddles that were in the tack room?" They were heavy for Logan to carry alone, but with his friend's help they could definitely be moved.

"We didn't touch them." Logan came farther in, relief on his face, and Martin followed.

At which point he saw why they'd been looking so guilty. Somehow they'd gotten into the paint he'd been using to touch up some fencing. They each had a white stripe down the backs of their shirts.

After he'd gotten an explanation—"we were playing skunk!"—and had taken the paint away from them, he set them to sweeping the barn floor under Cowboy's watchful eye while he took one last look around for the saddles. He didn't find them, and a couple of phone calls ascertained that no one else from the ranch had taken them anywhere. No adults, anyway.

Which meant this might very well be part

of the recent small acts of sabotage that had been plaguing the region.

He was just punching in a text to his friend Heath Grayson, a Texas Ranger who was spending his spare time investigating the sabotage problem, when a familiar pickup approached. Heath Grayson himself got out.

"Just the man I want to see." Flint pocketed his phone with the text message unsent.

Heath walked around the truck and toward Flint, holding up a cooler. The small bag on top of it produced a home-baked smell that made Flint's stomach rumble. "Josie heard Mrs. Toler quit," Heath explained, "so she sent over some of her famous mac and cheese for your dinner. Couple of giant chocolate chips cookies, too."

At that, Logan came running out of the barn, followed by Martin. "Cookies! Can I have mine now, Dad?"

Flint thought. It was four thirty, and he had another hour or more of work to do around here before he could take Logan home and start dinner. Or rather, heat up dinner, thanks to Josie and Heath's generosity. It was a long time for a hungry little boy to wait. "Sure. Say thank you to Mr. Grayson first."

"Thanks!" Logan said, his eyes widening as he took the big cookie Heath held out to him.

"That's big! Can I have some of it?" Martin asked.

"No way!" Logan turned away from the other boy.

"Logan." Flint squatted down in front of his son, who was holding his cookie to his chest like the other boy might grab it.

Which, judging from Martin's angry stance, might well happen.

"We share what we have," he told Logan. "That's what it means to be a friend."

Logan's expression was defiant, and worry pushed at the edges of Flint's mind. How did you make sure a kid grew up right? He knew how to get Logan to do his chores and follow behavior rules, but what about the softer side, things like being generous and helping others?

Things that mattered most of all?

Something one of Logan's Sunday school teachers had put into the church newsletter came to him. *Values are caught, not taught.*

He turned to Logan's friend, inhaled the chocolate chip aroma regretfully, and held out the cookie bag. "Here, Martin. You can have my cookie."

"Thanks, Mr. Rawlings!" Martin pulled the cookie out of the bag and took a big bite.

Heath was laughing. "You scored, Martin. That's Mr. Rawlings's favorite kind of cookie."

Logan looked briefly ashamed, then his face lit up with a new idea. "Let's climb up in the hayloft and eat them."

"Cool!"

They turned, and then Logan stopped and looked over his shoulder. "Is that okay, Dad?"

"Sure, if you take it slow up the ladder." Flint was glad to see Logan had asked permission.

"Can I go first?" Martin asked.

Logan opened his mouth, then shut it again, a struggle apparent on his face. He looked up at Flint.

Flint just waited.

"Yeah," Logan said finally. "You can go first."

Flint gave Logan a nod and a smile, and Logan's face lit up again.

As the two boys ran toward the barn, Cowboy racing in circles around them, Heath chuckled. "I'm taking notes." He'd just gotten engaged to Josie Markham, who'd been widowed right after discovering she was pregnant. Flint was pretty sure the wedding would happen sooner rather than later, because Heath wanted to help parent Josie's baby from day one.

"Notes might help, but nothing's going to prepare you for fatherhood. How's Josie doing?"

"Okay, except she wants to keep working as hard as ever, and at almost seven months pregnant, she can't do it all."

"Thank her for me." Flint gestured toward the cooler. "Logan'll be glad to have something that's not out of a box. And for that matter, so will I."

Heath chuckled. "I'd rather have an MRE than your cooking."

MREs. Meals Ready to Eat. The acronym, and the thought of military rations, brought back a wave of wartime memories for Flint, and a glance at Heath's face showed the same had happened to him.

They'd been through a lot together.

The awareness was there, but neither of them wanted to bring it up. Some memories were best left sleeping. "How's your grandpa?" Flint asked to change the subject. "Still planning a visit?"

Flint had helped track Edmund Grayson down last month. When old Cyrus Culpepper had left the Triple C to the Lone Star Cowboy League, his bequest had come with the condition that the other four original residents of the boys ranch be located and, if possible, brought to the area for the LSCL's anniversary celebration in March. The League was hard at work to fulfill the conditions so they could keep the boys ranch going strong.

Heath's grandfather, Edmund Grayson, was one of those original residents, and it had been Flint's responsibility to help find him. Which he'd done, with Heath's help.

"Coming out for Christmas, I think. And for sure to the reunion in March." Heath leaned against the fence surrounding the horse corral. "You said you wanted to see me about something?"

Flint pushed back his hat and leaned on the fence beside his friend, looking out over the land he'd come to love, brown grass of December notwithstanding. Then he hitched a thumb toward the barn. "Missing some saddles," he said, and told Heath what was gone and when he'd last seen them.

As Flint had expected, Heath got into analyzing the situation right away. During his enforced leave from his Texas Ranger job last month, he'd started digging into some of the recent problems in the area. Although he was back at work now, he'd continued to keep an eye on the situation. "You've got more valuable saddles they didn't take, right?"

Flint nodded. "Doesn't make a whole lot of sense." He waited for Heath to home in on the ranch boys as suspects. Flint was worried about that, himself. They were the ones who had the most opportunity.

All the more reason Logan shouldn't be over-involved with them. Flint would have to keep up the effort to recruit more varied after-school friends for Logan.

Heath was rubbing his chin, looking thoughtful. "Could be someone trying to pin a theft on the ranch boys, make 'em look bad."

Since Heath had only recently overcome his animosity to the boys ranch, his attitude pleased Flint. "Like who?" he asked. "Phillips?" Fletcher Snowden Phillips, local lawyer and chief curmudgeon, was forever criticizing the ranch for its supposed negative impact on property values and attracting new business.

"Could be." Heath plucked a piece of grass and chewed it, absently. "Could be Avery Culpepper, too. She's got some pretty strong opinions about the ranch."

Two of Flint's least favorite people. "You're right. Could be either one. Except I can't figure either of them getting their hands dirty, breaking into a barn and stealing saddles."

"Good point. Truth is, any lowlife who knows about the ranch might take kid stuff. Because they'd figure we'd blame the boys."

"Yeah, and those saddles do have some resale value." And Flint would have to replace them if they weren't found quickly.

"I'll take a look around," Heath said.

As they walked toward the barn, Flint's phone buzzed. He pulled it out. An unfamiliar number, but local. "I'd better take this," he said, gesturing for Heath to go ahead into the tack room. He clicked to answer the call.

"Mr. Rawlings, this is Lana Alvarez over at the school."

Flint stopped. Liking for her musical voice warred with a sense that, whatever Lana Alvarez had to say to him, it wasn't going to be good. "What's up?"

"I'm calling to request a conference. Could we set up a time for you to come in to school? I'm afraid there's a problem with Logan."

Chapter Two

The next afternoon, Lana Alvarez looked at the large school clock and frowned. Her nervousness was turning into annoyance.

Flint Rawlings was late.

"Still here?" Rhetta Douglass, the other first-grade teacher, stuck her dreadlocked head through the door and then walked in. "Girl, it's four fifteen on a Friday. This place is empty. Go home! Get a life!"

"Parent conference." Lana wrinkled her nose. If Rhetta only knew how little of a life Lana had, she'd probably laugh...and then invite her over.

Lana and Rhetta had both started as new

teachers this year, and they were becoming friends, but Rhetta had a husband and twin three-year-old sons. She didn't need Lana horning in on her family time.

Rhetta put down her bags, bulging with student work and supplies, and came over to perch on the edge of Lana's desk. "Who schedules a conference at four fifteen on the one day we're allowed to leave early? You better look out, or I'm going to sign you up for Cowboy Singles-dot-com."

Waving a hand back and forth and laughing, Lana leaned back in her teacher's chair. "Not going there. And I'm about to leave. I didn't schedule the conference for four fifteen. The parent is—"

At that moment Flint Rawlings appeared in the doorway, taking off his hat and running a hand through messy blond hair. "Sorry I'm late." His well-worn boots, plaid shirt and jeans proclaimed he'd come straight from the ranch.

Rhetta raised an eyebrow at Lana. "On second thought, you may not need that website after all," she murmured, and headed over toward her things. She waved at Flint as she walked out the door.

Lana crossed the room to greet Flint, hoping he hadn't heard that Cowboy Singles remark. "Come in, Mr. Rawlings." She led the way back through the classroom to the teacher's desk up front.

Although she'd already put an adult-sized metal folding chair beside her desk, anticipating Flint's visit, it didn't seem large enough for the rugged rancher. Maybe it was the fact that she was used to males of the first-grade variety, but Flint Rawlings seemed to overwhelm the room by his very presence.

"Thank you for—"

"I'm sorry about—"

They both stopped. "Go ahead," Lana said, gesturing for Flint to finish.

He shook his head. "Nothing important. It's just, we had a little episode up at the ranch. That's why I'm late. If you need to reschedule, it's fine."

It sounded like he wanted her to reschedule. Really? Wasn't he concerned about his son? "I think the situation is important enough that we'd better discuss it now."

"That's fine, then. What's going on?" He propped a booted foot on one knee and then set it down again. Like he was trying to get comfortable, or...

He wiped a bandanna across his forehead, and understanding struck Lana. He was nervous! The manly Flint Rawlings was sweating bullets in the classroom of his son's first-grade teacher.

It was a phenomenon she'd seen in her previous job, too. Lots of parents had anxiety around teachers, usually a result of bad childhood experiences or just excessive worry about their children. Whatever was the case with Flint, the realization siphoned off some of her annoyance.

She crossed her legs, folded her hands and

faced him. "So, we had some trouble with Logan yesterday."

"What sort of trouble?" He raised his eyes from the floor—or had he been looking at her legs?—and frowned. "If it was disrespect—"

"Not exactly. Hear me out." She picked up a pencil and tapped it on the table, end over end, eraser and then point. "During our one-on-one reading time, he refused to read. Just clamped his mouth shut and wouldn't say anything."

"That's funny." Flint looked puzzled. "He likes to look through picture books at home, and he's always pointing out words he recognizes on signs and such."

"I'm glad you have books for him at home. That's so important." She smiled at the man, wanting to put him at ease. "He usually enjoys reading here, too. He's definitely ahead of the curve in the subject. But yesterday, nothing."

"I'll talk to him." Flint scooted his chair back as if the conference was over.

She folded her arms. "There's more."

"What else?" he asked, visibly forcing himself to sit still and focus.

"After reading time, he knocked over a bucket of erasers." She nodded over to them, now neatly atop a stand beside the chalkboard. "He refused to pick them up. Just crossed his arms over his chest and shook his head. I thought about sending him to the principal, but—"

"What?" Flint half rose from the chair. "The principal? Why am I only now hearing about this?"

"I called yesterday," Lana reminded him, "and offered you a choice of conference times. This was the earliest one that worked for *you*." She emphasized the last word slightly.

"Right. Go on."

"After I kept Logan in at recess and talked to him, I decided I should get in touch with you before bringing the principal into the picture. Didn't Logan tell you about any of this?"

Flint shook his head slowly. "Not a word. Is that all?" He looked at her and sank back into the chair. "That's not all, is it." It was a statement, not a question.

"If that were all, I wouldn't have called you." This was the hardest part, but it needed to be said. "During our conversation at recess, he refused to apologize. I asked some questions, tried to figure out what was going on with him—because this behavior was pretty unusual for Logan—but he wouldn't answer. Until..." She paused.

Flint's blue eyes were on her. For better or worse, she had his attention now.

"He wanted to know if he was in enough trouble to be sent to live with the other boys at the main ranch house."

Flint closed his eyes for a minute and then opened them.

"When I said no, of course not, he burst into tears. He kept asking, 'What do I have to do to get to live there?'"

Flint stared at Lana, trying to conceal the emotions that were churning in his gut. Not only did he feel like a failure as a father, but he ached for his son.

What Logan really wanted was a mother, a family, company his own age instead of an elderly nanny who tried to get him to sit still and watch TV with her. He wanted attention, not constant scolding from his dad as he followed him around the barn, getting in the way and causing trouble.

Flint wanted those things for Logan, too.

But unfortunately for both of them, none of what Logan wanted was in the cards for him. Not now, and not in the foreseeable future. "I'll talk to him," Flint said as soon as he could control his voice.

"That's great, but I'm not sure it's enough," Lana said gently. "I might be able to help, if you can let me in on some of the things Logan's struggling with."

The sympathy on her face just made him feel worse. He hardened his voice. Toughened up his heart. "Bottom line," he said, "Logan's struggling with not having a mother. That can't be helped. And since his nanny quit, he needs something more after school."

Lana nodded, looking a little skeptical.

"I'm trying to find him some better play-mates," Flint defended himself. "And I've put out feelers about another nanny."

"I wonder if what he *might* need," she said, still sounding gentle, "is more attention from you."

That, on top of how stressed-out he already felt, made him mad. "I have a demanding job. I don't get off at three thirty like a teacher does!"

She looked pointedly up at the clock, now creeping toward five. "A teacher's work doesn't end when the students go home, but that's not the issue." She leaned back and looked at him narrowly, tapping a pencil on the desk. "May I be honest, Mr. Rawlings?"

"Doesn't seem like you have a problem with that."

"When it's called for. Mr. Rawlings, there were three children whose parents didn't come to Open House. Two were from migrant families who were trying to get here when their truck broke down on the road outside town. The other was Logan." She paused, letting that sink in good and deep, and then spoke again. "All three of them cried the next day when the other children were sharing about their families' reactions to Open House."

Flint just looked at her, absorbing the criticism in her words and her expression. *Yep, a failure as a father.*

"Now, I happen to know the ranch went on lockdown that night. I know there were problems with the boys, and you probably had to help. Logan knows that, too," she said. "In his mind, at least. But maybe not in his heart."

Flint let his head drop into his hands and stared down at the floor. He loved Logan more than he'd ever loved anyone, but according to Miss Lana Alvarez, he wasn't doing a very good job of showing it.

"The other two families who missed Open House got in touch to find out if there was another way to be involved with the school. I had one mother, who's a great cook, bring in *flan* for our Harvest Celebration. The other child's parents both work in the fields, possibly even longer hours than you work."

Was that sarcasm in her voice? He felt too guilty to be sure.

"But his grandpa, who's too disabled for farmwork, is helping me tutor the kids who need help in reading, one day a week before school."

He looked up at her then, spread his hands. "I'll talk to Logan about his behavior," he said. More like, talk *at* him. He needed to show how much he cared, not just lecture his son. "And I'll come to…whatever I'm supposed to come to, whatever you recommend, here at the school."

"We always need parents to help with holiday parties," she said, a dimple tugging at her cheek. "Ours is the last hour of the last day before Christmas break. But…I don't suppose you'd want to help with that. It would be a pretty demanding first activity with the kids."

Was she making fun of him or issuing a challenge? He narrowed his eyes at her. "You don't think I can do it, do you?"

She raised a very pretty eyebrow and shrugged, smiling openly now. "Let's just say the kids are pretty rowdy then. The parents who help have to plan a *lot* of activities."

Yeah, and he had no idea what kind of activities worked for first-graders, which was a pretty sad statement in itself, since he was the father of one.

But Lana Alvarez's amused gaze made him want to rise to the challenge. "You're on. When is it?"

"A week from Wednesday. Two o'clock."

He pulled out his phone and punched in the date and time, marking it "high priority."

"But meanwhile," she said, "he may need more attention at home than you're able to give him, with your responsibilities. I'll ask around and see if anyone knows of a nanny."

"No." Flint shook his head. "If he needs more attention, he can get it from me."

"If you're sure," she said in a voice that made it clear she had her doubts.

He really wanted to get out of here, but for Logan's sake, he forced himself to ask for help. "Is there..." He cleared his throat. "Is there anything I could do now to make it a little better? Show him I've at least seen his classroom?"

She tipped her head to one side. "Hmm. Want to leave a note in his desk for him to find on Monday?"

Logan would love that. Flint took the paper and felt-tipped pen she pushed toward him, jotted a quick note, and went to put it in Logan's desk.

On an impulse, he squeezed himself into the tiny chair connected to the desk and, holding his phone out, took a picture of himself.

"Logan's going to love seeing that," Lana said. "But I'm not sure you're going to be able to get out of there."

Sure enough, he had a hard time unfolding himself out of the cramped little desk.

When he stood up, she did, too, and he realized that her bag, bulging with papers, was packed and ready to go. He'd kept her at school overtime.

"Let me help you with that," he offered, holding out a hand.

She shook her head. "It's fine. I'm used to carrying it."

"That doesn't mean you can't accept a little help."

"It's fine," she repeated.

So the lady was independent. Didn't want help.

Or maybe she just didn't want help from him.

They walked together through the deserted hallways. Outside, the sun was setting in a bank of pink-and-gold clouds. His truck was the only vehicle left in the parking lot. "I'm sorry I kept you late," he said, "and I appreciate your taking the time to meet with me. Where's your car?"

She clapped a hand to her forehead. "In the shop, and I forgot about it. I was going to grab a ride with Rhetta." She shrugged. "Oh, well, I need the exercise. See you soon, Mr. Rawlings. Don't hesitate to contact me if you have any questions."

"You can call me Flint," he said, "and I'll give you a ride home. Where do you live?" He remembered someone telling him that Lana had grown up around here, and he wondered if she lived with her folks.

"Call me Lana, and I'm not going home. I'm going to the church."

"On a Friday night?" That surprised him. He would've thought someone as pretty as Lana would have her choice of dates. What was wrong with the cowboys around here?

Seeming to read his line of thought, she blushed. "I'm not much for the roadhouse or the karaoke place. And a lot of my friends are married and home with their families so I…" She trailed off, looking away with a forced laugh. "What can I say? I've spent the last three Friday nights helping Marnie Binder sort stuff for the Christmas bazaar."

Flint filed that away, trying to ignore the pleasure her words gave him. No reason for him to care what Lana Alvarez did with her evenings. Pretty young women were poison to him.

But on the other hand, Lana sounded a little lonely. And he'd care about any lonely person; he had that much Christian faith left. "What about your folks? I thought you grew up around here."

"They're gone. Car accident when I was a teenager. It's just me."

"I'm sorry." Her matter-of-fact tone tugged at his heart. Lana Alvarez was even more alone than he was. And she seemed like a family type. Good with kids. She ought to be happily married, not heading off to church alone.

"Come on," he said. "I'll drive you to the church. I have a few things to drop off for the Christmas bazaar, myself."

Lana found the ride to the church a little awkward. Partly because this handsome man had discovered that she had no dates and no exciting social life, and he was clearly surprised. He probably found her pitiful.

He must have found their silence awkward, too, because he flipped on the radio. She was expecting country music, but to her surprise, the sound of a classical violin concerto filled the cab of the truck.

"Vivaldi?" she asked, recognizing the tune from her music history course in college.

He glanced over at her and nodded. "Calms me down," he said a bit sheepishly.

"Does that, too?" She pointed at the baby picture of Logan that dangled from his key chain.

He glanced down at it, and his jaw tightened. Which was a weird reaction to a picture of one's child. Most people gushed about such precious mementos.

Not Flint. "That's to remind me to keep my priorities straight," he gritted out.

"Oh?"

"Yeah." He reached over and turned up the radio, his eyes firmly on the road.

Well, okay then. Lana turned and looked out the window, pretending great interest in the brown grass and blue sky, and then in the storefronts that dotted Haven's tiny downtown.

When they pulled up to the little white church, Lana hurried to get out of the truck before Flint could open the door for her, but her heavy bag of paperwork made her lurch awkwardly as she tried to climb down from the high cab. Flint was there instantly, steadying her with a hand on her elbow. He didn't let go until she was safely on the ground.

She pulled away, her heart thudding ridiculously. What was *wrong* with her?

He reached for her heavy attaché case. "I can carry that."

"No, it's fine." She kept her hold on it. Even gave it a little tug.

He let go but studied her for a moment like she was a puzzle he needed to solve. "Okay, Miss Alvarez." Then he walked around to the back of the pickup and pulled out a large wood beam. He hoisted it to one shoulder. "Ready?"

Wow. He was strong. "Sure. Do you want me to…need me to carry something?"

He gave her that puzzle-solving look again. "Yeah, pick up that other beam, would you?"

She turned, stood on tiptoe and peeked into the bed of the truck, where another large beam rested. It had to weigh over a hundred pounds. She glanced at him. Was he serious?

A smile tugged at the corner of his mouth. "That was a joke, Lana. Come on."

A joke. He'd made a joke.

She held the doors for him to carry the

beam inside. When they reached the church's fellowship area, Marnie Binder was bending over a box of colorful fabric. She straightened up and shook back her gray curls, her face breaking into a wide smile. "Well, look there," she said. "Two of my favorite people in Texas, coming in together."

Lana smiled, put down her things, and submitted to the woman's big hug. As the ranch cook and an active volunteer in the church, Marnie mothered everyone. She and Lana had gotten close quickly when Lana had returned to town. Since Marnie had no kids and Lana had lost her mother, the relationship suited both of them.

Lana admired the craft kits Marnie was making for the younger kids at the craft bazaar and laughed at the older woman's description of talking a shop manager into giving her scrap fabric for free.

Flint set down the beam and disappeared, returning a moment later with the other beam on his shoulder, stacking it beside some other building materials in one corner of the hall.

Marnie surveyed them both fondly. "I'm so glad you two are dating. This is nice! Where are you headed tonight?"

"We're not dating!" Lana exclaimed.

"I just gave Lana a ride," Flint said quickly.

Her face felt hot. She couldn't look at Flint. For some reason, Marnie's mistake was hard to laugh off.

"I'm outta here." Flint lifted his hands and took two steps back. He sounded just as embarrassed—and uninterested—as Lana was herself.

Talk about a blow to the ego.

"You'll make sure she gets home all right?" Flint asked Marnie in a gruff voice, once he'd gotten to the doorway of the big room. "Her car's at the shop."

"Of course." Marnie gave him a knowing look. "That's sweet you're so protective."

Flint lifted his eyes to the ceiling, turned around, and left the church.

The moment he was out the door, Marnie clapped her hands and turned to Lana. "I don't know why I didn't think of it before," she said. "You two would be perfect together! Both single, both good-looking, both responsible adults. You love children, and Flint needs someone to help with Logan. You're both—"

"Marnie! Stop!" Lana waved her hands to halt the flow of words. Now that Flint was gone, she could laugh. "That's completely ridiculous."

"Why? He's a good, churchgoing man. At least..." A rare frown crossed the woman's face.

"What?"

"I'm trying to think when it was that Flint came back to church." She started sorting paintable wooden Christmas ornaments into bins, looking thoughtful. "You know, I think it was when Logan got big enough to notice. For a while after his big trouble, when Logan was a baby, Flint stayed away from church. But that was understandable."

Lana knew she shouldn't ask, but she couldn't resist being interested in the gruff cowboy's history. "What was his big trouble, anyway?"

"You haven't heard?" Marnie shook her head, clucking her tongue. "What a shame. That young wife of his. If I'd seen her leaving, I'd have stopped her and knocked some sense right into her head."

"Leaving Flint?"

"And her newborn baby. No sooner had she recovered from childbirth than she was out of Haven, and hasn't been back since."

"Oh, wow!" Lana stared at Marnie. "Doesn't she even see Logan?"

"Nope."

"That's awful!"

"I know." Marnie put down a wooden ornament extra hard, making a loud *thwack*. "Wants nothing to do with him, apparently. I just don't understand that. I was never blessed with children, but if I had been, you can be sure I'd never leave them feeling un-loved, like that poor Logan."

"How could she *do* that? Logan's the sweet-est kid around, and Flint..." She trailed off. Flint certainly wasn't a talker, and maybe he was rough around the edges, but he seemed basically kind and protective. Wouldn't any-one want to stick together with someone like Flint?

Marnie gave her a sly look. "Yes, speak-ing of Flint. He's handsome, isn't he? Even my niece, who's sixteen and hates everyone, calls Flint a hottie."

"He *is* good-looking," Lana admitted.

"So, you should think about going out with him."

Lana made a big time-out sign with her arms. "Not me. He may be a hottie, like your niece says, but I don't like hotties."

"Why not? Oh." Understanding dawned on Marnie's broad face. "I heard something about your, um, engagement."

Lana couldn't help the surge of heat that rose in her cheeks. "It's all right. You can say it. I'm sure everyone in town knows." Restless, she started moving paintbrushes from one can to another. "It happened more than six months ago. I should be over it."

Marnie came around the table and put an arm around her. "Getting left at the altar must have been a real big hurt. I'm so sorry it happened to you."

Lana held herself stiff for a minute, but Marnie just patted her shoulder and kept on hugging, and finally, Lana let herself be comforted. Somehow, Marnie knew just what she needed.

Lana's girlfriends had been mad on her behalf, and the relatives who'd helped plan the wedding had gotten busy handling everything, sending the guests home, donating the food to a local homeless shelter, taking down the decorations.

Everyone had been kind to Lana, sympathetic, but in passing. No one knew quite what to say to a jilted bride.

But now, tonight, Marnie's sympathy was all for her, and Lana let herself cry a little on the older woman's comfortable shoulder. When she'd settled down, Marnie urged her into a chair and brought her a cup of tea.

"I'm sure it was awful and embarrassing." Marnie brought a couple of Christmas cookies from the church kitchen and put them on a napkin in front of Lana. "But you'll move past it."

"It's not an easy thing to get past," Lana said, and blew her nose.

"There, now. Eat a cookie. That's right. Those middle-school students won't miss a couple of cookies. The ladies made enough for an army."

Lana sipped tea and wiped the mascara from beneath her eyes. "Sorry, Marnie. I'm sure you didn't expect your Friday night to involve counseling."

"Not the first time." Marnie patted her

hand. "God's house is a good place to work through your sadness and get a new perspective. You can get over this, Lana. You can find love again."

Lana broke off a piece of cookie and crumbled it over the napkin. "Not going there again. I'm a disaster with men. I'm too needy."

"You're the opposite of needy! You're always doing for others. And anyway, you're way too young to decide on a life of celibacy."

"I may be young, but some things, I know."

"You've had a lot of losses for someone so young," Marnie said, studying her thoughtfully. "You had to learn early that nothing in this world is permanent. And that's true. We only see through a glass darkly, like the good book says. But that doesn't mean we shouldn't enjoy this life and the people around us."

Lana smiled at the woman who was trying so hard to comfort her. "I do enjoy the people around me. I love the kids. And I'm blessed with friends like you."

"And the Lord meets your basic needs, right? Better than any human. But still…" Marnie sighed and put a hand over her heart. "There's nothing like the love of a good man."

Lana wouldn't know, but her friend's comment reminded her to get out of her own concerns. Marnie was a widow and had had plenty of losses herself. "Tell me about Oscar," she said. "That was your husband's name, right?"

And looking at the pictures Marnie pulled up on her phone, listening to the stories of storms they'd weathered, vacations they'd shared, the home they'd built together, made Lana feel the tiniest spark of hopeless longing. Maybe there was a small chance that someday, somehow, she'd find love herself.

Maybe even with someone a little bit like Flint Rawlings.

But, no. No way. He was cranky, struggling to care for his son, emotionally repressed. A heartache waiting to happen.

The sound of organ music drifted from upstairs, along with some laughter; musicians practicing for Sunday's service, no doubt. Lana breathed in the piney scent from evergreen branches brought in to decorate the church and drank down the rest of her tea, warm and comforting with its hint of lemon and mint.

She busied herself with pushing boxes of glue and scissors and sewing supplies across the room and carrying heavy containers of donated items out from the storage closet. She worked up a sweat and tried not to think.

An hour later, after they'd finished their work and were leaving the church, Marnie stopped still. "I just had the best idea."

"What's that?"

"Did you hear that Flint Rawlings's nanny quit this week?"

"Uh-huh."

"Well, *you* should become Flint Rawlings's temporary nanny!" Marnie's face broke into a broad smile. "Sometimes, I'm a genius."

"Marnie! Would you stop with the matchmaking?"

"No, I'm serious. School's almost out, right? And I've been worrying about how you're going to spend the holidays, alone as you are. You could spend time at the ranch, help a little boy who needs it, and, well, just be a part of things. A ranch at Christmas is a wonderful place."

Marnie's words created a vision inside Lana. Having people around her at Christmas, gathering around the table or the fire, helping out Logan…seeing Flint on a daily basis… "No. That wouldn't work."

"Why not?"

"Just…it wouldn't, okay?" All of a sudden, Lana felt like the church was too warm and small. She needed air. "You know what, I think I'm going to walk home, all right?" Without waiting for Marnie to answer, she hurried out of the church, bag in hand, and strode rapidly in the direction of her lonely little apartment where fairy-tale dreams wouldn't disturb the small, safe life she was trying to build for herself.

Chapter Three

The next Monday, Flint was teaching three of the teenagers how to take apart and grease a balky hay baler when he saw the elementary school bus chugging toward the ranch.

"Stick with it," he told them, "and help Ben get up to speed, okay?" He was glad that Ben Turner had joined the group. The boy wasn't always so good with social interactions. But to his surprise, Robby Gonzalez and Ben were hitting it off, which was good; they both needed a friend.

Flint jogged up toward the ranch house, Cowboy trotting alongside, tongue hanging out. They arrived in time to meet Logan as he came off the bus.

He was starting to get the hang of this single dad stuff. After his conference with Lana Alvarez last week, he'd made a commitment to himself to spend more quality time with Logan.

Logan's coat was half on, half off, and Flint knelt to adjust it as Logan talked a mile a minute. "How'd you put a note in my desk, huh, Dad? That was cool!"

Flint pulled out his phone and showed Logan the picture of himself sitting in Logan's place at school. "I wanted to see your classroom, buddy. Pretty neat desk you keep."

"Oh man, that's cool!" Logan started pulling papers out of his backpack. "Look, Dad! I got a star *and* a sticker on my Write-and-Draw!"

Taking the paper, Flint examined the carefully formed letters that spelled out "Dad" and "Logan." Logan had drawn a small figure and a larger one, hand in hand, at the top of the sheet.

Flint's throat tightened. He'd made some mistakes in his life, but Logan had come out of one of them. Maybe God knew what He was doing after all.

"And Miss Alvarez wrote you a note, too! Only I can't read it." Logan pulled out a sheet of note paper with a border of colorful crayons and a couple of sentences of neat handwriting, and thrust it in Flint's face. "What does it say, Dad?"

Flint read it aloud: *Logan was very cooperative today about doing his reading and cleaning up his part of the classroom. He's excited to have his dad help at the Christmas party.*

"Yeah!" Logan yelled. "Miss Alvarez said I did good! And—" he cocked his head to one side "—she even said you're going to come help with our party."

Flint nodded. "That's the plan."

"Will you know how to do it, though?"

Logan asked doubtfully. "Like, to make crafts and stuff?"

"I'll figure it out," Flint promised.

"Okay." Logan accepted Flint's word without question, making Flint doubly determined to shine as a school dad.

They walked beside the main ranch house together, heading for the barn. As Logan chattered on about his day at school, Flint's mind wandered to Lana Alvarez. It had been nice of her to send home some positive reinforcement, both for his sake and for Logan's. She was a good person. He'd thought about her a number of times since their conference and then dropping her off at the church.

In fact, it was hard to get her *off* his mind. But as for Marnie's talk about their dating—which the inquisitive, good-natured cook had brought up again to him, twice—no way. No *way*. Lana Alvarez was the last woman he'd want to date. Even if she weren't Logan's teacher, she was way too young and way too pretty. In other words, way too much like Logan's mom.

As they passed the parking lot behind the ranch house, a car door slammed, and Avery Culpepper sauntered forward, a plate of cookies in her hand.

Who had she come to see? He wasn't aware of the newcomer having any friends at the ranch. She'd done a better job of making enemies. Yes, she was Cyrus Culpepper's granddaughter and heir, but the fact that her grandfather had left her only a small cabin and a bit of land had made her bitter. She'd threatened to contest the will, get control of the ranch and sell it off. Her plan, if she was able to go through with it, would ruin a lot of boys' opportunity for a second chance, but that didn't seem to bother her. Her latest stunt had been to try to pressure the Lone Star Cowboy League, who controlled the ranch, into giving her a large amount of money to prevent her going to court.

Not a nice woman. "Can I help you?" he asked, stepping in front of her.

"Sure, cowboy," she said, raising her eyebrows and tossing back her brassy-blond hair.

If that was supposed to have an effect on him, it didn't work.

Logan was another story. He stepped toward her with a winning smile. "Those cookies smell good!"

"They *are* good," she purred, squatting down in front of Logan and waving the plate in front of him.

"Can I have one?" Logan started to reach for a cookie.

Avery pulled the plate back. "Not so fast. Are you one of the, ah, *troubled* boys?"

Logan looked up at Flint. "Am I, Dad?"

"No." He leveled a glare at Avery. "I can deliver those to the residents if you like." *After checking them for cyanide.* Since when did Avery Culpepper give a hoot about the boys who lived here?

"No, that's all right," she purred. "I'm sure

you have all kinds of big, important things to do." She shot him a challenging stare. "While you can."

So she was still bent on destroying the ranch. At least, that was how *he* interpreted her remark.

Which made her gift of cookies seem like a ploy rather than a charitable gesture.

"Come on, Logan." He didn't want his son anywhere near this woman.

"But, Dad—"

"Now."

"Listen to your daddy, little boy," Avery said, dismissing Logan with a wave of her fancy pink-fingernailed hand.

Logan trotted after Flint and, when he caught up, shot a resentful look back over his shoulder. "She didn't even give me a cookie, Dad. And what's 'troubled' mean?"

"We'll talk about it later. Nothing to worry about."

"She's pretty, but I don't like her."

"Neither do I." None too soon for Logan to

learn that "pretty" didn't necessarily mean kind or worth getting to know. That it was actually, usually, something to watch out for. "Come on, you can play with Cowboy and the barn kittens while I finish working with the older boys."

Lana pulled into the ranch house parking lot just in time to see Logan and Flint turn away from Avery Culpepper and head toward the barn.

She got out of her car slowly, watching the pair. Flint had slowed his strides to match Logan's, and Logan was obviously chattering a mile a minute.

"Cute, aren't they?" Avery Culpepper approached and nodded toward Flint and Logan, a catlike smile on her face. "Do you have a thing for the ranch manager?"

Lana's face heated. "No! Logan's in my class at school—"

"And he's *almost* as cute as his daddy."

Avery frowned darkly. "Too bad Flint's involved with that Lone Star Cowboy League."

Rumors of Avery's beef with The League had circulated around church and school, but Lana didn't know enough about it to take sides. "The league does a lot of good," she said mildly.

"So they claim." The woman's mouth twisted.

"O-kaaay." Lana didn't know how to respond to that. "I'd better get to my tutoring. The boys are probably waiting."

Lana headed toward the ranch house, Avery falling into step beside her. Jagged thoughts pierced Lana's contentment in the midst of a peaceful day. What had Avery and Flint been talking about? Was Avery interested in Flint?

Was Flint interested in Avery? She didn't seem like his type, but you never knew with men. Even those who seemed to hold admirable values could end up letting you down.

Lana drew in a breath and looked skyward, centering herself. It didn't really matter if Flint and Avery were interested in each other, because she, Lana, wasn't going to get involved with any man. She'd tried and failed. She just wasn't good at dating, love, relationships.

It wasn't in the cards for everyone, getting married. And she had plenty to do, and plenty to be thankful for, without being on the arm of a man.

"So how are you liking life in Haven?" she asked Avery, determined to be cheerful.

The woman laughed without humor. "It's not what I'm used to."

"Oh?"

"I'm more of a city girl. Grew up in Dallas."

Lana nodded. "I lived in Austin for a while, during college and for a couple years afterwards. It was fun to have so many choices about what to do." Although Lana was perfectly content with a small town now. When one of her college teachers had recommended her for a job in the city of Dallas, she'd thanked him—but inside, she'd known she wouldn't consider it.

"Yeah, instead of sitting home all weekend, or going to the same two bars and seeing the same people."

Lana laughed. "I can relate. Well, not to the bars, but I sit at home too much." She felt like she ought to propose they get together, but the truth was she didn't feel very drawn to Avery. They probably didn't have much in common.

Still, the woman was new in town and seemed lonely.

Inspiration hit. "Would you like to come to church with me next Sunday? I haven't seen you there."

"Me? Church?" Avery looked sideways at her.

"Sure! We have a very welcoming, warm congregation. It's a great place to make friends."

Avery sighed dramatically. "Maybe church

would be good for me. I'm...I'm just so sad lately."

"I'm sorry." They'd reached the point where Lana needed to head toward the library, but instead, she turned to Avery. "Are you okay? Do you want to talk about it?"

"No. There's nothing you can do." Avery looked off into the distance, brushing her fingers under her eyes. "It's just hard that I never got to know my grandfather. Maybe if I'd grown up here, I'd understand the people and feel more a part of things."

"That *is* sad."

Avery shrugged. "When you grow up in foster care, you learn how to make the best of things."

Sympathy twisted Lana's heart. She'd had a warm, loving family herself—up until the accident—so she felt for people who hadn't been so fortunate. "I really hope you'll come to church on Sunday," she said, patting Avery's arm. "I'll give you a ride."

At that minute, Marnie Binder came out

of the main ranch house's back door, letting the screen slam behind her. She approached Lana and Avery, stopped, and put her hands on her hips. "What are you doing here?" she asked Avery.

"I thought I'd like to look around," Avery said. "And look, I brought some cookies for the boys."

"We have plenty of cookies already," Marnie said. "And if you want to look around, you need to take it up with Beatrice Brewster. She's the ranch director." Marnie turned and stomped back into the house.

What was that about? In the months Lana had known Marnie, the woman had never been anything but kind to others.

Avery looked annoyed. "What's *her* problem? Can't a girl do a good deed?" She thrust the cookies into Lana's hands. "Here, send these along to the boys. I'm going to take a look around the ranch. *Without* anyone's approval."

Avery headed off in the direction of the

barn, leaving Lana thoroughly confused about who Avery was and what she was looking for.

In front of the barn, Flint, Robby Gonzalez and Ben Turner had just gotten the harvester back together. They fired it up and listened to the newly smooth sound of the engine. While the boys high-fived each other, Flint felt an uneasy prickle in the back of his neck.

He turned around. He hadn't seen Logan in a while, but he was probably still content in the barn with the new kittens and a video game.

Somewhere behind the barn, Cowboy was barking as if he'd cornered a cat.

Avery Culpepper came from the same direction as Cowboy's commotion, heading toward one of the older boys who'd been helping with the harvester before, Stephen Barnes. What did she want with him? Stephen was supposed to go home for good at Christmastime, and all the staff was hoping he could keep it together and get along with his stepfather well enough to make it happen.

A moment later, a shout from the other direction spun him around.

And then a familiar, high-pitched scream. Logan. The voice sounded like Logan.

Flint was running before the sound died out, running toward the other side of the barn. As he came around the corner, horror struck him.

One of the open-air tractors was rolling down a slope with Logan at the wheel.

Dimly aware of Cowboy loping beside him, barking, Flint ran faster, his eyes on the drama still half a football field's distance away from him. Panic hammered at his chest.

Logan's mouth was open, and he was screaming. He held on to the wheel, but clearly more to keep from being thrown out of the tractor than because he could control its direction. And now Flint realized that Robby Gonzalez ran beside him, yelling something about the brake.

Could Logan even reach the brake? Flint forced his arms and legs to pump faster, at the same time trying to calculate what had happened. Logan must have knocked the tractor out of gear. And the vehicle was headed toward a metal gate. If the tractor hit it, Logan would go flying. Might be badly hurt, even—

Robby took a flying leap, trying to grab on and climb into the driver's seat with Logan, but his foot slipped, and he fell backward with a yell. Cowboy raced ahead and reached Robby's side.

"Get help!" Flint roared at Ben Turner as he passed the boy, his heart and lungs burning, running faster than he'd ever run in his life.

The tractor was picking up speed, and if Logan tried to jump...

"Stay there, Logan!" he yelled, jumping over sagebrush and dodging clumps of grass. "Just stay! I'm coming!"

Behind him he heard shouting, a commotion, but his focus remained on one thing:

Logan. Flint was gaining on the tractor now. He couldn't let it hit that gate.

All thought left him, and he was just a body, running as he'd run in wartime, even faster, because it wasn't just any life at stake, it was his son's.

A prayer sprang from deep inside him: *Help us, Lord!*

Somehow, he found his timing and took a flying leap into the tractor. He grabbed Logan in one arm and the steering wheel in the other, slid his feet into place and hit the brake.

The tractor jolted to a halt, jerking both of them hard.

And then everything was still.

Gasping for air, his heart pounding like a posthole digger, Flint pulled Logan onto his lap. Reached down and put the tractor back in gear. Set the brake. And then brushed Logan's hair back and studied him, checking for damage.

Logan seemed to catch his breath again

then, and he started to cry. A normal, scared-kid cry. Not an "I might get killed" cry.

Praise the Lord.

Blessed. Just for this one moment, he and Logan had been blessed.

"I was scared, Daddy!"

Flint held his son in his arms and sent up a prayer of thanks. His son was safe. He had a second chance.

His heart still pounded so hard it felt like his chest would explode. Delayed reaction nerves had his hands shaking.

He pulled Logan close against his chest. "Never scare me like that again, buddy."

Logan rubbed his face on Flint's shirt. "I'm sorry."

Ben and several of the other boys from the ranch arrived at the tractor, with Marnie and Lana Alvarez close behind them.

"What happened?" Lana asked. "Is Logan okay?"

"He's fine." Flint didn't even have it in him to feel ashamed that the teacher had seen his son in danger. He was still too shaken, too thankful that Logan was alive.

But not too shaken to check for other casualties. "Is Robby all right?" he thought to ask. "He did his best to try to help. Took quite a fall."

"I'm fine," the boy said, stepping out from the little crowd. "Sorry I couldn't stop the tractor."

"Mr. Rawlings flew!" said one of the other boys.

"Come on," Marnie said, taking charge. "Let's get Logan inside. I've got a plate of cookies with his name on it. Homemade by *me*," she added, with a dark look in Avery Culpepper's direction.

Flint realized then that Avery hadn't joined the crowd around them. She was disappearing over the hill, in the direction of the parking lot. Weird.

So they all walked back toward the ranch house together. For the teenage boys, the situation had evolved into something cool, and they traded stories about what they'd seen, how Robby had tried to jump on the tractor, how Ben had run race-pace to get help.

Marnie was still muttering about Avery. "I wouldn't doubt if that woman had something to do with this," she said.

Flint was holding Logan, focusing on him, but he had to correct that unfair accusation. "She wasn't anywhere near, Marnie. I'm pretty sure Logan brought this on himself, playing with the gears on the tractor." He eyeballed his son. "Right?"

"She didn't touch the tractor..."

"What?" Flint snapped to attention.

"Miss Culpepper didn't touch it," Logan repeated. "She just told me if I climbed up she'd take my picture."

"I knew it!" Marnie's hand went to her hip. "I'm going to have a word with that girl."

"Get in line," Flint said.

Lana put a hand on both of their arms. "I'm sure she didn't mean for all of that to happen.

And we need to keep the focus on what's most important." She nodded toward Logan.

"Am I in trouble?" Logan asked, sniffling.

How did you discipline a kid when his whole life had just flashed before your eyes? Flint schooled his features into firmness. "One thing's for sure, tractors are going to be off-limits for a long time."

Logan just buried his head in Flint's shoulder.

As they all started walking again, Flint felt that delicate hand on his arm once more.

"You doing okay?" Lana Alvarez asked.

He shook his head. "I just got a few more gray hairs. I should've been watching him better."

"Maybe so," Marnie said. "But you can't, not with all the work you have at the ranch. So I think we can all agree—you need a babysitter for Logan." She stepped in front of Lana and Flint, causing them both to stop. "And the right person to do it is here. Miss Lana Alvarez."

"Oh, Flint doesn't want—"

"You've got time after school. And a Christmas vacation coming up." Marnie crossed her arms, looking determined. "Logan already loves you. You could help to keep him safe and happy."

Flint's desire to keep Lana at a distance tried to raise its head, but his worry about his son, his gratitude about Logan's safety, and the sheer terror he'd just been through, put his own concerns into perspective.

Logan took priority. And if Lana would agree to be Logan's nanny on a temporary basis, that would be best for Logan.

And Flint would tolerate her nearness. Somehow.

"Can she, Daddy?" Logan asked, his face eager.

He turned to Lana, who looked like she was facing a firing squad. "Can you?" he asked her.

"Please, Miss Alvarez?" Logan chimed in.

Lana drew in a breath and studied them

both, and Flint could almost see the wheels turning in her brain.

He could see mixed feelings on her face, too. Fondness for Logan. Mistrust of Flint himself.

Maybe a little bit of…what was that hint of pain that wrinkled her forehead and darkened her eyes?

Flint felt like he was holding his breath.

Finally, Lana gave a definitive nod. "All right," she said. "We can try it. But I'm going to have some very definite rules for you, young man." She looked at Logan with mock sternness.

As they started walking toward the house again, Lana gave Flint a cool stare that made him think she might have some definite rules for him, too.

Chapter Four

As Lana pulled up to the ranch the next day after school, she saw Flint waiting for her. Arms crossed, big like a mountain.

Her heart pounded way harder than it should. What had she gotten herself into? Why had Flint's problem, how to take care of his son and give him the attention he needed, somehow become her problem?

As soon as she parked and got out of her car, he approached her. "We need to talk," he said, "before Logan gets here."

"Sure. He's riding the late bus, right?" She'd brought a bag with a change of clothes, and she pulled it out of her backseat. "By the way, the terms you texted me last night were more than adequate."

"I've been thinking since then," he said. "Give that bag to me. Let's walk and talk."

"Being a foreman means you're bossy, I guess?" She let him take the bag out of her hands, because it seemed like it wouldn't do much good to argue.

One side of his mouth quirked up just a little. "Maybe. Come on. I want to show you something." He shepherded her toward the rear of the ranch house.

His hand on the small of her back meant nothing, she reminded herself as he ushered her through the kitchen. Just another piece of his bossiness. But the unseasonably warm weather made her fan herself and inch away from him as they arrived at a room in the back. Actually, a little apartment.

"We got to thinking," he said. "Marnie and Bea and I. We wondered if you'd want to stay here through the holidays."

"Stay here?" She looked around the cozy little efficiency. "Why? I have a place in town."

"True, but sometimes, I have to work late. Mrs. Toler used to stay over, but it wouldn't be appropriate…" He trailed off.

Lana swallowed.

"Anyway, it's inconvenient having to bring clothes along each day, isn't it?"

She turned around, looking at the apartment. "It's true I haven't really settled my place yet," she admitted. The small apartment building where she lived in Haven had been a temporary solution when she'd gotten the teaching job in August. And she'd been feeling depressed about being there alone over the holidays. To live at the ranch, surrounded by all the kids and clutter and life… It would definitely suit her.

"See, there's a desk and study lamp." He turned it on, then off again. "For your teacher work. The place isn't fancy, but…"

The door to the apartment burst open, and Bea Brewster, the fiftysomething director of the boys ranch, came in. Tall, with no-nonsense brown hair and glasses, she was stern and fair. The boys all knew they couldn't pull anything over on her. And everyone learned pretty quickly that there was a heart of gold beneath her businesslike facade.

"Just the two people I want to see," she said. "Do the two of you have a moment? Did I hear, Lana, that you might stay with us for a while?"

Lana blinked. "I…I might. Flint suggested the idea just now. Is that what you wanted to talk about? If it's a question of rent, I'm month by month at my apartment…"

"No. No rent." Bea patted Lana's shoulder. "It's just standing empty. You're one of our best volunteers. Take it."

"But someone else might want—"

Bea waved a hand. "All of our other volunteers have…" She paused, her mouth quirking as if she was embarrassed. "No one else needs it."

Heat rose in Lana's face. She knew exactly

what Bea had been about to say. *All of our other volunteers have families.* She took a quick glance at Flint. Did he think she was pitiful, all alone in the world?

He was looking at her thoughtfully, but exactly *what* he was thinking, she couldn't tell.

"Now," Bea said, "I want to talk to the both of you about the Christmas pageant."

Lana couldn't restrain a little hand clap. "I remember those from growing up around here. They were wonderful. You're still doing them?"

"Well," Bea said, "I hope so. The community loves it, the boys love it…" She waved an expressive arm back toward the rest of the ranch house. "We all love it. But with the move and all it entails, I just don't have time to do the pageant justice, and it's floundering for lack of leadership. We're in a new venue, and we need new ideas. Lana, would you consider taking charge of it?"

"I…" Lana gulped. "When is it?"

"It's in exactly ten days." Bea sighed.

"Next Friday night, which doesn't give us much time. I have the scripts, and the parts are assigned, but I haven't done much more than that. You can rehearse the boys over the weekend and after school, and once they're off, they can rehearse all day if you want them to."

"It sounds like you have it organized pretty well," Lana temporized, wondering if she could possibly make the time to do it. "It's true I did community theater when I was growing up."

"Then you'll do it?" Bea asked, smiling as if she already had Lana's answer.

Lana felt overwhelmed, but she also wanted to help. "I'll give it a try. Just show me where the materials are, and the scripts, and the assigned parts, and...I'll take it from there."

"Thank you!" Bea pulled her into a hug. "You're such an asset to the ranch. Now, Flint." She looked at the big rancher, who'd been standing off to the side in his quiet way. "I think it would be best to do the pageant in the storage barn. We'll let some of the older boys off their regular chores to help clean it, and the Macks have agreed to supervise that, since several of their boys will be involved." She turned to Lana. "The Macks—Eleanor and Edward—are our house parents in Wing One."

Lana nodded. "I've met them."

"Someone will need to build the sets." Bea looked up at Flint. "I know you're busy, but you helped last year, so you know what's involved. Are you willing to spearhead that part?"

Lana's stomach danced with some strange kind of butterflies. She was already going to be spending time with Flint, as Logan's nanny. If he helped with the pageant, that would be even more togetherness. And the fact that she felt more excited than upset was bad news.

She did *not* need to get a crush on the ranch foreman. Anything remotely resembling love meant heartbreak. She'd seen that all too clearly. "I'm good with a hammer," she offered, giving Flint a way out.

"I'm sure you are, dear," Bea said, "and resourceful to boot. But you'll have your hands full with the boys."

"I'd like to help." Flint spoke slowly. "But I've recently realized—" he glanced at Lana, then back at Bea "—that I'm not giving Logan the time he deserves. I hesitate to take on another commitment that would pull me away from him."

"But that's the beauty of this assignment." Bea raised a hand for emphasis. "Logan has a part in the pageant, and I'd like all the boys to be participating in the set building when they're not practicing their parts. The more skills we can give them, the better, and it's a chance to develop their work ethic. So you'd actually be spending *more* time with your son."

Flint chuckled and raised his hands like stop signs. "Okay, okay. Can't say no to

Miss Bea," he said to Lana. "As long as I can spend time with Logan, I'll help."

From the direction of the ranch house's kitchen, a crash sounded. A boy's voice raised, then Marnie Binder's exclamation, then another crash.

"I'd better see what that's all about," Bea said. "Thank you both, so much, for agreeing to help. Flint, could you show Lana the barn so she knows what she's dealing with?"

"Uh, sure." He rubbed the back of his neck. Bea rushed off, and Lana leaned back against the study desk, propping her hands on either side of herself. "My head's spinning," she admitted to Flint. "Did I just get a new place to live and a second new job?" Then realization struck her, and her hand flew to her mouth. "I didn't even think of how this could interfere with being Logan's nanny. I'm sorry. I can turn it down."

Again, the little half smile quirked Flint's mouth. "No, you can't," he said. "Nobody turns Bea down for anything. And it'll be fine for Logan, since he's involved in the pageant."

"You're sure?"

He nodded. "And if you're serious about staying out here, me and some of the guys can help you move in whatever things you need for the holidays. Tomorrow, if you'd like."

"Whew." She mentally cataloged the time remaining in the week. "Maybe Thursday evening would be better."

"All right. Let's take a look at the barn." Without waiting for her, he led the way out of the ranch house.

Lana followed along behind him, her thoughts racing. Just last week, she'd been looking toward the holidays with dread, unable to muster the energy to decorate her bare little apartment. In fact... She stopped still.

Of *course*.

She'd prayed for God to get her through the holidays in good spirits, giving her a way to help others in order to escape her own loneliness. She'd envisioned God bestowing some sort of meditative peace where she didn't feel the loneliness so badly. She'd hoped He'd block from her mind the fact that she was supposed to be celebrating her first Christmas as a newlywed, help her bear her solitude with grace.

She'd never considered that God would answer her prayers in a completely different way. A way so much better than giving her a quiet, calm peace. A way filled with fun and energy and kids and friends. A way exactly perfect for who she was.

Thank you, Father. She looked up at the blue sky and involuntarily lifted her hands in praise and thanksgiving.

When she started walking again, she saw Flint looking at her quizzically. "You okay?"

"I'm great," she said, smiling and hurrying to catch up with him. Clearly, the Lord was guiding her through this Christmas season. And if He'd given her a cross to bear in the form of a very handsome cowboy, well, He was known for that sort of thing. With His help, it would all turn out okay.

After Flint had shown her the barn, Lana went to meet Logan and then shooed Flint away, assuring him that she could find her way around the cabin with Logan's help.

A cross to bear was one thing, but being in Flint's company for the entire afternoon was too much.

So she followed the exuberant Logan along the dirt road to the little cabin where he and his father were living. Beside them, a breeze rustled through the milo stalks, making them rattle. Ducks, a small flock of them, whooshed off the small lake and into the sky, quacking. The winter sun warmed Lana's back.

"Come on, it's this way!" Logan ran ahead with his usual high energy, clearly proud to have been given the responsibility of show-ing his new nanny the ropes. He trotted up the front porch steps of the little wooden cabin and jumped on the sturdy porch swing to wait for her.

She walked more slowly to study the place where she'd be working. A star emblem was carved into the rough-wood siding, centered near the roof. Window air conditioners assured comfort when the Texas heat got too extreme. No flowers, and the porch wasn't personalized with any homey touches. Lana wondered whether that was because they'd moved in recently or because Flint wasn't the homey type.

"Here's our kitchen and living room," Logan explained, holding the door for her as she walked inside and then running after her, letting it bang behind him. "And here's where Cowboy sleeps." He knelt beside the plaid dog bed adjacent to the couch, rearranging the dog's toys inside.

Lana looked around at the simple appliances, woodstove, couch and chairs. A fleet of small trucks littered the rug, and a book lay open beside the big chair and ottoman. A Western, Louis L'Amour. So that was Flint's spot, and she couldn't be surprised at his reading material. He was a cowboy to the core.

"C'mon, I'll show you my room!" Logan charged up to the loft area, and she followed, curious. The loft split into two sections, one on the right side of the staircase and one on the left.

She followed Logan to the left side, where bunk beds, cowboy sheets and a little stack of books signaled a young boy's room.

Logan gestured toward the other side of the loft, accessible by a narrow passage along the railing. "Want to see Dad's room?"

"No, it's okay." Though she was curious about how a cowboy decorated. Probably a saddle blanket for a bedspread and a log for a nightstand.

Or maybe it wasn't really decorated at all. Logan's room wasn't. "You have a lot of boxes," she said, indicating the neatly stacked row along one wall.

"Yeah. We didn't have time to get out my stuff yet. I have a lamp and some more toys and some old clothes from when I was little. Mrs. Toler was supposed to help unpack them, but she was always too tired to come upstairs."

"Well, maybe you and I could do that sometime."

"That would be great!" he shouted. Then his face fell. "Only, don't open *those* boxes." He pointed toward a stack of nine or ten cartons near the walk-in closet Flint and Logan apparently shared. "Those are my mom's things."

"Oh." Lana tried not to show her surprise.

"I didn't even know we had anything from my mom," Logan confided, "but when we moved, we found these. I...I got in trouble."

Lana didn't want to pry, but she sensed that Logan needed to talk about this. "Did you do something against the rules?"

"I didn't know it was a rule," Logan explained, "not to get in those boxes. So I did, and I found a bunch of old pictures of Daddy. He was all dressed up in a fancy suit. And there were a bunch of other people in the pictures, and a lady with a fancy white dress. She was real pretty." Logan sighed.

"And that was your mom?" Lana asked, her heart aching for the little boy.

"Yeah. I never saw her before. She had long blond hair like a princess."

"I'm sure she *was* pretty, because you're a good-looking boy." She ruffled Logan's hair. She wondered if she should talk to Flint about the importance of letting Logan know something about his mother. He shouldn't feel like the topic was forbidden. He should be allowed to have a picture of the woman who'd given him life.

And yet, she reminded herself, she didn't know the whole story. And she wasn't family. She was just the teacher and, for a little while, the nanny.

"Show me your books," she suggested as she kept thinking about the situation. Why was Flint so sensitive about his ex-wife that he forbade his son to even open the boxes related to her…and yet, he kept those boxes around? Was he hung up on his ex? Praying that she'd return someday? Or hopelessly angry and bitter?

But there was no reason to be curious about Flint, Lana reminded herself. It wasn't as if she were looking for a boyfriend; but if she had been, he obviously wasn't a good choice. Too much emotional baggage.

So she turned her attention to Logan. They read a couple of his favorite books together, and when he questioned some of the facts in his Texas nature book, they went outside to identify trees and grasses and bugs. When an armadillo crossed the dirt road in front of them, Lana encouraged Logan to try to get close. It was a way for him to run off some energy, and he'd never be able to catch the heavily armored creature, which, according to the book they'd been looking at, could run up to thirty miles an hour.

Finally they headed back inside, Logan still panting. "Are you going to cook dinner, like Mrs. Toler did sometimes?" he asked.

"I don't know." Lana and Flint had only talked about her duties with Logan, but she could see now that the two of them needed a little household help, as well. And she was feeling blessed with the chance to spend time with Logan, with the Christmas pageant and with her new place to stay for the holidays. "Let's see what you have in the refrigerator, okay?"

It took some searching, but they found the makings of chili. No tortillas, but Logan produced some tortilla chips that would do. Lana let Logan dump cans of beans into the pot and showed him a few rudiments of measuring and fractions in the process. The side dish had to be fruit from cans, and when Logan found some marshmallows, it turned into an ambrosia salad like Lana remembered loving when she was a kid.

While the chili cooked and sunset made the sky into a work of art, Lana and Logan cuddled up on the couch and read stories, waiting for Flint to come home. And Lana felt a very, very dangerous contentment.

"Come on, Cowboy." Flint whistled to the dog as he climbed out of his truck. "Let's get some grub and some rest." It had been a long day, longer than he'd expected. He was looking forward to collapsing into his chair. Except that he'd have a hungry kid and an annoyed nanny to deal with first, if past experience was any indication.

Although Lana Alvarez was about as different from Mrs. Toler as day was from night. He found himself whistling as he strode up the steps to the porch.

He opened the cottage's front door and stopped, dumbstruck at the scene before him.

Clearly, Logan had been sitting in Lana's

lap listening to a story when they'd both nodded off. Now, Lana leaned sideways against
the back of the couch, her legs covered with
a fleece blanket. In her arms was Logan,
curled up, his fist pressed to his mouth as it
usually was when he slept. A Christmas storybook lay open on the floor.

Soft carols played on the radio. There was
an unbelievably good smell coming out of
the kitchen.

His chest ached with wanting the unre-
alistic thing his senses presented to him.
What would it be like to come home to such
a scene every night? Did guys who got to do
that realize how good they had it?

Self-protective armor slammed over the
top of his longing. Deliberately, he banged
the door behind himself, making a wake-up
noise. "What's going on here?"

Cowboy bounded in and jumped up at the
pair on the couch, front paws propped, tail
wagging, barking.

Lana's eyes opened and then went wide as

Logan stirred in her lap. She sat up and slid her bare feet to the ground. Blinking, hair mussed, face pink, she still kept her arms around Logan, checking to see that he was steady before letting go.

Flint sucked in a breath and turned away, busying himself with taking off his dirty boots.

"Quit it, Cowboy!" Logan scrambled down to the floor, only half-awake, wrestling with the barking, prancing dog.

When Flint straightened up again, Lana was standing, too, brushing back her hair with spread fingers.

"Whoa," she said, shaking her head a little. "I'm sorry I fell asleep. Logan, did you sleep, too?"

"Yeah!" He rolled on the floor with the dog, laughing.

"I better check the chili." She hurried into the kitchen, still without looking at Flint.

Flint's heart rate had slowed down a little. "You must have done a lot of running around with Miss Alvarez, huh, buddy?" He sat down on the floor beside Logan and Cowboy. Ever since Lana had dressed him down about Logan's need for more attention, he'd been looking at his own habits. A little boy needed his dad after work.

So Flint had been trying to sit with Logan for a few minutes after they got home each evening, rather than getting right into cooking dinner.

Only maybe he didn't have to cook dinner tonight, because the smells from the kitchen were fantastic.

"Hey, your dinner is ready when you are," Lana said, coming out of the kitchen.

Logan sat up. "I helped make dinner, Dad!" he said. "And we measured stuff and Miss Alvarez said it was math!"

"That's great, buddy." He stood and approached Lana. "I didn't mean for you to do my cooking."

"It was no problem. I enjoy it." She picked

up her jacket and purse. "Logan, I'll see you at school tomorrow."

Logan frowned. "Where are you going, Miss Alvarez? It's time for dinner. We have to see if the chili is too spicy. And which fruit salad Dad likes best, the plain or the fluffy."

"You can tell me tomorrow." She patted Logan's shoulder.

"You cooked it. You should stay to eat it." The words coming out of Flint's own mouth surprised him; up until one second ago, he'd meant to tell her to go on home. Having Lana stay to dinner put Logan at risk of caring too much, of expecting things he couldn't have.

"Please, stay, Miss Alvarez." Logan leaned against her, looking up with wide eyes.

"Well…" Lana gave Flint a helpless look.

He couldn't help smiling. He'd never met a woman who could resist Logan's smile and puppy dog eyes—well, except for Avery Culpepper—and he had the feeling Lana Alvarez wasn't an Avery kind of woman.

He ought to help her with an excuse if she wanted one. "Hey, buddy. Miss Alvarez might have other plans." He didn't want her to have other plans, but he knew that if she did, that would be best. Despite her lack of a date last Friday night, he'd seen the cowboys looking. If she didn't have a boyfriend now, it was only a matter of time until she did. There were plenty of willing candidates right here on the Triple C.

She met his eyes, and the corners of her mouth quirked up in a rueful smile. "Plans to make lesson plans, that's all. I guess I could stay for a quick bite."

The gladness that lifted his spirits worried him.

Logan didn't have any such concerns. "Yay!" he yelled, hugging her. "Come on, let's eat!"

In a few minutes of working together, they got dinner on the table. Flint had forced himself to forget the good feeling of being at home with a woman, the rightness of breaking bread together. But it came right back to him, even though he didn't want to reawaken that awareness in himself, and he definitely didn't want to stimulate it in Logan. The boy was already longing for things he'd never have.

When he tasted the chili, though, he thought the emotional consequences might be worth it. "Food's good," he said, too engrossed in scooping it up to say more.

"Better than what Dad cooks," Logan volunteered, slurping loudly from his spoon.

Lana smiled. "That's good to hear. Any self-respecting Mexican should be able to make a good chili. My mom would be very upset if I didn't live up to the family tradition."

"How long has your family been in this area?" Flint forced himself to slow down on his eating. He knew Lana had lived around Haven growing up, and she had no trace of a Spanish accent, but from her name and coloring, he assumed she was full-blooded Mexican.

"My parents and grandma emigrated thirty

years ago." She smiled, her eyes going dreamy like she was remembering something good. "My parents took pride in the fact that I was born here."

"Where's your mom and dad, Miss Alvarez?" Logan asked around a mouthful of chili. "Are they old people?"

"They died in a car accident," she said matter-of-factly.

Logan's eyes widened.

Flint put a hand over his son's. Given the world today, it was never too early to model the right words to say in the face of a sad situation. "We're sorry for your loss."

"Thank you." She smiled reassuringly at Logan. "It happened ten years ago, and I have a lot of good memories."

"And the rest of your extended family?" Flint asked.

"Still in Mexico." She propped her cheek on her hand. "That's the disadvantage of our family moving here. I don't really know my Mexican relatives well. We went to visit a few times when I was smaller, but Mom and Dad got very busy in the community here, and we stopped making the trip."

"Is your grandmother…" He hesitated, not wanting to overemphasize death around his son.

Lana glanced at Logan and shook her head, obviously on the same page with Flint about protecting Logan from too much scary information.

"So…you're alone." Sympathy, something he didn't feel too often toward women, nudged at his heart.

She nodded. "I mean, I have friends. But the holidays can be sort of hard. What about you, Flint? You're not native to this area, right?"

He shook his head. "I grew up in Colorado. Me and my eight brothers."

Her eyes widened. "Eight brothers? That's a whole baseball team!"

He chuckled. "That's right, but growing

up on a farm, we didn't have much time for baseball."

"Why'd you leave?"

He shrugged. "I was a younger brother. I'd have liked to live on the family farm, but by the time I was of age, my older brother had already claimed it. Which is good," he added to forestall pity. "He's made a go of it. Anyway, by the time I graduated from high school, there wasn't money for college, so I went into the army. That way, I'll have the GI bill when—if—I ever decide I want to get a degree." He spread his hands. "For now, I know how to be a soldier, a farmer or a rancher. That's it. So when I heard there was a job open here, I applied and got it."

"Do you miss Colorado?" she asked.

"I don't miss the snow, but I do miss my brothers."

"We go see them every summer," Logan volunteered as he grabbed another handful of tortilla chips. "We climbed a mountain and went on a roller coaster."

"That's right, buddy, and we'll do it again this year."

"That's nice," Lana said. "You and Logan aren't such a small family after all."

"But, I don't have a mom," Logan said. "Like we talked about." He gave Lana a meaningful look.

Logan had talked about his lack of a mother with Lana?

"We didn't look in the boxes," Logan announced, looking at Flint worriedly.

Flint blew out a breath. He wasn't proud of how he'd responded when Logan had come to him with the wedding album Flint hadn't even known he still had. Usually, he avoided thinking about his ex-wife. But Logan was getting to an age where he obviously had questions. Flint needed to figure out how to answer them, but not tonight and not in Lana Alvarez's presence.

They ate the fruit salad—they all preferred the fluffy version—and then Logan went and leaned against Lana's side. "Can you stay and watch a movie with me and help me go to bed?" he asked, looking up at her with a pleading smile.

Whoa. Not good. Flint hardened his heart. "No, buddy, Miss Alvarez has to go home."

"I can't, but I'll see you tomorrow," she said at the same time.

She stood and started carrying dishes to the sink, but Flint rose quickly and raised a hand. "I'll take it from here." He needed to get Lana Alvarez out of his house. He had to remember that a pretty, too-young woman who looked like a dream come true when she woke up wasn't any part of his life, nor his son's. That, in fact, she was more dangerous than a lightning storm to both of them.

Chapter Five

Lana pushed back a stray curl, looked around at the not-very-clean storage barn filled with shouting boys and milling adults, and fanned herself with the Christmas pageant script. *Why did I agree to do this again?*

It didn't help that she'd come straight from a full day of teaching first-graders who were hyperexcited about Christmas. Nor that she hadn't slept much last night, since scenes from her evening with Flint and Logan kept replaying themselves in her mind.

Pastor Andrew tapped her on the shoulder, and she turned. He was here to help organize the gifts that community members always donated for the boys, and she figured that the lanky young man wanted information or help from her. Instead, his eyes were warm with sympathy. "Want me to settle everyone down with a prayer?"

"That would be wonderful. Thank you."

The pastor boomed out a call for attention, put a hand on Lana's shoulder, and prayed that the pageant would bless the community and bring people comfort and peace. Which put the focus right where it should be, on helping others rather than worrying. "Thank you," Lana said, giving the pastor an impulsive hug.

Then, before the air of spiritual peace and thoughtfulness could dissipate, she started organizing everyone into groups, putting older boys in charge of younger ones and pairing experienced adult volunteers with novices.

Pastor Andrew took charge of noting down the gifts people were dropping off for the boys at the ranch.

Marnie Binder came through the door just as Lana was trying to figure out what to do with a group of teenage girls from a service club at the local public school. Ostensibly here to help, they were actually more of a distraction to the teen boys. Instantly, Marnie read the situation and pulled the girls aside to help with decorations.

When Lana checked in with the set-building group, off at the far end of the barn, there was Flint. The way he looked at her made her feel flustered. Had he been able to read her mind last night? Had she accidentally revealed how much she enjoyed being at his house, pretending to be part of a family?

It's just pretend, she reminded herself firmly, and refocused on the multiple tasks at hand. As soon as she'd ascertained that Flint knew exactly what to do and that he was already adept at delegating the right task to the right boy, she turned away.

As she headed back toward the youngest group of boys, whose rehearsal of lines under

Robby Gonzalez's leadership seemed a little chaotic, she was surprised to see Avery Culpepper come through the barn door, talking on her cell phone. When the blonde saw Lana, she clicked her phone off and approached her like they were old friends. "Hi, Lana! I wanted to see if I could help with the pageant."

"We need all the help we can get." Lana studied the woman, looking for signs of insincerity. Ever since the near-accident with the tractor, she'd been curious whether Avery had played a role in it.

She looked around, trying to think of a safe place to put Avery to work, when Robby called to her for help, laughing: *"¡Ayúdeme!"*

She hurried over, Avery trailing behind.

"We want to know if Mary and Joseph were married." Logan was obviously the spokesperson for the first-grade boys.

"Yeah," added Colby, the nephew of Lana's friend Macy. "They had a baby."

The next group over was listening, and one

of the teenagers chimed in. "You don't have to be married to have a—"

"Jesus was the son of God," Lana interrupted, holding up a hand to quell the older boy's remark. "And Mary was his mother." She looked around and noticed that a number of the other groups had stopped working to listen in on the discussion. Including Flint's group. *Great*.

But of course, Flint would want to know how his son's religious education was being handled. What he might not know was that kids asked every kind of question, including questions that were inappropriate or hard to answer.

"What about Joseph?" Logan asked, looking puzzled. "Wasn't *he* Jesus's daddy?"

Eleven-year-old Jordan Gibson, one of the new residents, leaned forward, arms crossed over upraised knees. "Joseph was like his adopted dad."

"Exactly." Lana smiled approval at Jordan.

"Hey, we should have Joseph and Mary's

wedding at our pageant!" eight-year-old Jasper Boswell shouted. Which led to a vigorous debate between the boys who thought a wedding pageant would be cool and the boys who thought it would be dumb.

Above the din, Avery's higher voice sounded loud and clear. "Miss Alvarez wouldn't want a wedding in the pageant." She waited until the noise died down. "That's a sore subject for her because of how she was, you know, left at the altar."

Avery's words hit Lana like a sudden blow to the chest. Her face heated, and tears sprang to her eyes. Every single person in the barn—or at least, it seemed like everyone—stared at her.

She should have brushed off Avery's remark with a joke, made everyone comfortable again. Only she couldn't think of a thing to say. Would she ever get over being mortified about her disastrous almost-wedding?

"Kids." Marnie Binder, who'd been standing in the barn doorway, clapped her hands.

"Break time. Cookies and hot chocolate on the ranch house porch."

Amid the shouting, running boys, Lana saw Flint approach Avery and escort her to the door of the barn, his face unsmiling, talking more than she'd ever seen the cowboy talk before.

Macy, who'd been helping Colby out of his costume so he could join the rest of the boys, finished quickly and hurried over to put an arm around Lana. "Come on. Help me find some supplies over in the library."

Because she didn't know what else to do, Lana left the barn with Macy. She took deep breaths of the soft evening air and wrapped her arms around her middle.

Once they were out of earshot of everyone else, Macy hugged Lana. "I'm so sorry that happened," she said, keeping an arm around Lana as they walked slowly toward the ranch library. "What is wrong with that Avery Culpepper, anyway?"

"How did she know?" Lana's voice came

out husky, so she cleared her throat. "It's not like my wedding disaster happened here in Haven. It was a couple hundred miles away, where my...where *he* was from."

"She's been sticking her nose into everyone's business in town. No doubt she asked the right question of someone who'd heard the story and didn't mind gossiping about it."

Lana breathed in and out a couple more times and managed a laugh. "She certainly brought the rehearsal to a halt."

"Maybe that's what she wanted." Macy frowned and held the library door for Lana to walk in ahead of her. "She's the type that likes to stir up trouble. Sometimes, I wish I hadn't located her." Macy was the one who'd contacted Avery and let her know her long-lost grandfather had passed away.

As they walked through the nearly empty library to pick up poster board from the little office, Lana noticed an old photograph with a prominent label: Culpepper Family. She paused to look at it, but Avery wasn't there; it was just Cyrus, his wife, June, and their son, John.

She studied the photo. "That's strange," she said, beckoning Macy over. "Avery's so fair, but all of her Culpepper ancestors have dark hair and eyes."

"Avery's hair color doesn't exist in nature." Macy came over to look at the picture, her arms full of poster board and other craft supplies.

"Here, let me carry some of that." Lana took a big box of scissors and glue out of Macy's arms. "You're right, I guess, but she's really fair-skinned, too. Blue eyes. Are you totally sure she's Cyrus's long-lost granddaughter?"

Macy shrugged as they exited the library. "It's an unusual name. There were just four Avery Culpeppers in the US, and our Avery was the only one in Texas. I left a message for her, and she got back to me a few hours later and said Cyrus was her grandfather."

"Did you get any documentation that she's who she says she is?"

"She showed us her driver's license. And I think there might be more paperwork coming, only it got delayed because of the holidays."

"I'm sure you're right. Maybe it's just because I'm irritated with her that I'm hoping we have the wrong person."

"Believe me, with all the trouble she's stirred up, I'd be happy to find out she was an impostor," Macy said. "Now you've got me wondering."

"I think I'll do a little digging after Christmas. Maybe I'll find a different Avery. A nicer one."

"Sure, go for it, though I don't have much hope. But look, maybe she'll leave town of her own accord." Macy nodded toward the parking lot. Avery was stomping off to her car, her face scrunched with either anger or tears. Flint stood at the edge of the parking lot, arms crossed, shaking his head.

Lana wondered what he'd said to Avery. Had he just chewed her out for her role in Logan's accident, or had he saved a little bit of energy to scold her for humiliating Lana in front of a barn full of people?

"Hey, listen, before we go back inside, sit down with me a minute." Macy called out to a couple of teenaged boys who were heading back from the house and asked them to carry the supplies inside. Then she led Lana to a wooden bench along the side of the barn. "We never get much chance to talk, but what happened today made me think. How are you doing about the whole broken engagement thing?"

"You can say it like it is," Lana said. "I was jilted at the altar."

"Well, right, which must have been awful. Are you starting to get over it, though?"

Lana shrugged. "Getting over Gregory wasn't actually that hard."

"You don't regret not being married?"

"To Gregory? No." Lana looked down at

her jeans, running a thumb over a torn spot in the denim. "I should have realized he wasn't ready to be married. I just wanted a family so bad that I overlooked the signs."

"You're not the first woman who's made a mistake in love," Macy said. "Maybe God helped you by having Gregory back out at the last minute."

"Maybe He did. But I wish He didn't give his lessons so harshly." Lana looked up at the darkening sky. "But who am I to question God? I didn't listen to my friends when they warned me about Gregory. I was sure he was the one."

"Sometimes God has to use a two-by-four," Macy said.

"That's right. But I learned my lesson."

"I'm sure you did. You'll make a better choice next time."

Lana opened her mouth to say there wouldn't be a next time and then closed it again. She didn't need another lecture on how she was too young to give up hope. For whatever reason, it made people uncomfortable when a woman her age said she was through with love.

So she stood. "We'd better get back to work," she said, and walked with her friend back into the barn.

Flint showed two of the teenage boys how to use sandpaper to smooth out the rough edges of the sleigh they were making. Then, after checking on the progress of the boys who were pounding nails into a stable rafter prop, he settled down to do some sanding himself.

Working with wood—and working with kids—helped his blood pressure settle back to normal after his confrontation with Avery Culpepper. Although they'd started out having a calm discussion, it had gotten heated when he'd brought up Logan and the tractor—and chewed her out for embarrassing Lana. When he'd told her in no uncertain terms to stay away from his son and stop causing trouble at the ranch, she'd gone stomping off even madder.

Which wasn't necessarily good for the boys ranch or the Lone Star Cowboy League.

Mostly, he hadn't liked her upsetting Lana.

Why that was his business, Flint didn't know. Lana was his son's teacher and temporary nanny, but otherwise not even a friend.

If that's the case, why'd you like having her at your house so much?

He shook off the thought. He'd be concerned about any acquaintance who'd been embarrassed like that. And naturally, a little curious. He didn't know what the story was about the wedding. Flint wasn't a person people tended to share gossip with.

Whatever had happened, there was no call for making Lana almost cry when she was working her fingers to the bone for this ranch.

"Hey, Dad, Robby says I know my part, so I can come help with props."

"Great." Flint started to nod toward the

area where the other younger boys were cutting black paper silhouettes, and then stopped. He was supposed to be spending time with Logan, bonding with him. "Come over here," he said. "Sit down with me, and I'll teach you how to sand."

"Cool!" Logan dived into the task with his usual enthusiasm. He emulated Flint exactly, and soon was sanding like a pro.

Flint's heart squeezed with love for his son. Whatever else he thought of Lana Alvarez, he was glad she'd called him to task for neglecting Logan. Since he'd started focusing more on his son, their relationship felt different.

Not only that, he realized, but Logan hadn't run away once.

After Logan went to find out what the other boys his age were doing, Flint looked up from his work and noticed Lana kneeling down over a bunch of gift-wrapped presents, her dark hair gleaming as she spoke with the preacher. Looked like they were figuring out what gifts went with what boys. She spoke a few minutes more, looking out at the room, nodding toward one boy and then another. The preacher said something that made her laugh, and then Lana stood and walked over to the makeshift stage, gesturing toward a group of boys to come rehearse with her.

The preacher watched her the whole way. Smiling.

Flint scolded himself for noticing. What man wouldn't want to watch Lana, share a joke with her? She was a beautiful woman, inside and out. A beautiful *young* woman, he reminded himself. Closer to the preacher's age than to his.

When Heath Grayson and Josie Markham came over, Flint was glad for the distraction. "What are you two doing here?"

"Stopped by to bring the gifts we're donating." Heath gestured back toward the stack of wrapped gifts, which had grown noticeably just over the course of the afternoon rehearsal.

"I'll put you to work," Flint offered, holding up a hammer.

"You stay," Josie said to Heath. "I'm going to find something else to do."

But the young boys from Flint's group stopped her. "Hey, Miss Markham," Logan said. "You and Mr. Grayson are like Mary and Joseph."

"Oh, really?" Josie sank down onto a bale of hay, moving a little awkwardly, and smiled at the boys. "Why's that?"

"'Cause you're going to have a baby," little TJ Johnson explained, "but you're not married."

Josie blushed and opened her mouth, then closed it again.

"But Mr. Grayson is gonna marry you. That's what *I* heard," added another boy, Damon Jones, who'd just come to the ranch last month.

Logan frowned. "But God was Jesus's dad." He looked up at Josie. "Is God your baby's daddy, too?"

"Logan," Flint scolded. "Ms. Markham doesn't need a lot of questions. That's not polite."

"It's okay." Josie looked up at Heath, who was trying hard not to laugh, and then smiled down at Logan. "My baby's daddy is my husband, Mr. Markham, who died."

"But Mr. Grayson is gonna take care of her and the baby, just like Joseph did." Damon was nodding thoughtfully.

"You could be Mary and Joseph in our pageant!" someone suggested.

Flint figured Heath and Josie had been on the spot enough. "Boys, let's get back to work," he said.

He watched as Heath helped Josie get up off the bale of hay. It was nice to see his friend looking at Josie that way, so possessive and caring, but it made Flint aware of all he was missing in life. He envied Heath, but he'd never marry again himself. One try was enough. He looked over at Logan, safe and happy, teaching the other boys to sand.

Logan had to be his focus. And if his heart ached a little every now and then, seeing what he couldn't have, well, life was like that. You didn't get everything. You were just grateful for what you had.

A few minutes later, Heath came back over and squatted down beside Flint. "Nice work."

"Not done." He handed Heath a pair of pliers. "Here, make yourself useful. Bend down the wires on those boards so nobody gets hurt."

Working together was comfortable. They'd done a fair amount of that before. "How's the ranger work going?" he asked Heath. "Glad to be back at it?"

"Yeah."

"Any news on the sabotage?"

"It's a mystery. Heard there was some more trouble over at McGarrett's place. Haven't had time to look into it."

"Avery Culpepper?" Flint measured the width of a board.

"I don't know. We were in town shopping

right before we came out here and saw Avery driving toward the Blue Bonnet Inn, looking mad as a wet cat."

"I could have had something to do with that. She was out here causing trouble, and I had words with her."

Heath shook his head. "Like it or not," he said, "she's got some power over us. If she goes through with that lawsuit, all this could go away." He gestured around at the noisy, happy scene.

"Irks me." Flint pounded a nail extra hard. "Why a woman like that should have power to destroy—"

"I didn't say she had power, not yet. Things may work out. But some say she's teaming up with Phillips."

"Heard that. Wouldn't be good."

They worked for a while longer, side by side. Heath showed some of the boys how to work with pliers, and then got caught up in telling stories about being a Texas Ranger. Which was good. The boys needed to have something to aspire to. Once Heath's stories shifted over to military life, Flint joined in. Some of the boys weren't going to have the resources to go to college right away—like he hadn't himself—and the military was a good option for them. More structure and discipline couldn't hurt, especially with boys who'd had a rough road growing up.

Heath finally stood and looked across the room, at which point Flint realized Josie was calling him. Man, he was attuned to her. It *was* like she was carrying his baby.

Or more like, he loved her.

As his friend threw an arm around his wife-to-be, Flint felt a little left out. What was that old country song about all your rowdy friends settling down? Not that he and Heath had ever been all that rowdy, but they'd been through a lot together. And until recently, Heath had shared Flint's desire to stay single.

Obviously, that was gone.

Flint scanned the rest of the room, and his

eyes settled on Lana, just as she approached the table where people had been labeling gifts. Someone said something to her and handed her one, and as he watched, Flint made out that the gift had her name on it.

She smiled and started to put it aside, but the person who'd handed it to her said something, and she laughed and opened it.

For whatever reason, Flint decided he needed to stretch his legs and strolled over closer, covering his curiosity with getting a water bottle from the case beside the door.

"What is it, Miss Alvarez?" a boy asked.

Several people turned to look; Flint wasn't the only one.

She pulled out a tin cross on a chain, then a brochure of some sort.

"Hey," Josie said, "we saw that show. Are there tickets?"

"No," Lana said, looking curious. "Just the brochure. I've been wanting to see this show."

"And you like a cross, too," Josie said. "Looks like you have a secret Santa."

"Is there a note?" someone asked.

Lana looked into the box and found an envelope. She opened it, read the note inside, and then looked around, her face skeptical. "Where's Pastor Andrew?"

"He left," Josie said.

Macy Swanson came over, and the three women put their heads together over the gift and note.

Flint turned away.

So the pastor was sweet on Lana. Planning to take her to a show in Dallas, and apparently Lana was game.

Well, that was good. A useful warning to him.

A woman like Lana—young, pretty, appealing—wouldn't last long in Haven. She'd want bigger and better things. Just like Logan's mother, she'd take the next train out of town when there was a new opportunity.

Or a new guy.

Flint walked over to the door of the barn and looked out into the deepening twilight.

Listened to the sound of an owl hooting in a nearby tree, of the creek rushing by. Smelled the hay that had been cut just today.

This was the world he had for himself and his boy, and it was enough. It was safe and secure. There were good people here, friends, folks who'd help him look out for Logan.

Longing for more was just stupid. Falling for a pretty young woman, even stupider. He'd been fooled once, and he couldn't let himself be fooled again. Not just for the sake of his own heart, but for Logan's.

He turned back into the barn and went back over to the sets project, keeping his face steadily turned away from Lana Alvarez. Keeping his distance.

But keeping his distance turned out to be harder than Flint had expected. Especially when he'd promised to help her move her things out to the ranch.

She'd tried to insist that she could do the work herself, could fit what she needed into her car, but Flint had been raised better than that. You didn't stand by while a lady did a bunch of physical labor.

Not that women weren't capable. Someone like Josie Markham proved that every day, working like a ranch hand while being seven months pregnant.

So he didn't stop Lana from carrying boxes down to his truck; he just made sure she had the lighter ones.

"Want me to box up the stuff from your fridge?" he asked, opening it.

She came and looked over his shoulder. "Now you've found me out. There's nothing perishable inside." She grinned at him. "I'm not exactly Susie homemaker."

"You cooked a mean chili," Flint said.

"I can cook," she said. "In fact, I like to. But there's nothing lonelier than eating by yourself. I end up over at the pizza place or Lila's Café pretty often."

"Now you can eat at the ranch." Flint hoisted a box containing coffee, tea and snacks. "Logan and I usually get at least one meal a day there. Marnie makes a pretty good lunch."

"I'm looking forward to that. She said I could help in the kitchen." That made him pause and lean against her counter. "You're going to wear yourself out with helping people," he said. "Don't you ever take a break?"

A pretty flush crossed her face. "I like to keep busy."

"Sure, me, too, but what you do puts just about everyone else to shame."

She turned away, her face closed. "Are we ready to go?"

"Sure." He waited while she locked up and then held the door for her. She got in like a queen, but didn't say one more word to him the whole ride to the ranch.

As they pulled onto the dirt road that led to the Triple C, he had to speak up. "Was there something I said that offended you, back there?"

"I just…you don't know what it's like to

be alone in the world, so don't judge how I cope with it, okay?"

Flint stopped the truck, frowning. "It's true, I have family and Logan. But don't underestimate other people's loneliness. It's possible to be lonely as a single parent, or among a big crowd of married family members. Or in a marriage, for that matter."

She arched an eyebrow at him. "Voice of experience?"

"Yeah."

Their eyes met, and there was compassion and understanding in hers, and he was pretty sure his own eyes reflected the same. They were two people who'd known loneliness and lived through it. Were still living through it.

Wouldn't it be nice if…

No. Flint halted his own urge to lean toward her, to brush back her hair, to kiss that sad look off her face. Lana Alvarez might want comfort, but he wasn't the man to provide it, and it was best to remember that.

"Come on," he said, opening his car door. "Let's get you moved in."

Even as he said it, he realized that he was moving temptation that much closer to himself and Logan.

Chapter Six

Early Sunday morning, curled up in an armchair in her new apartment, Lana finished her morning prayers and set aside her Bible. Then she jumped up and went to her closet to pick out clothes for church.

The red dress, that would be Christmassy.

But she felt uneasy, and a moment's reflection told her why. She had a little unfinished business to do first. She needed to text Avery Culpepper and let her know that she wouldn't be picking her up for church as planned.

Avery couldn't still be expecting a ride from Lana, could she? After publicly humiliating Lana about her wedding, surely she'd found another ride or decided not to go. Lana would just text her to confirm.

She swiped through her contacts, found Avery's number and opened a text message box.

Her thumb over the keyboard, she paused. Maybe it was too early to text Avery. She'd wait until after getting dressed.

She slipped into the dress, grabbed her hairbrush and brushed her hair, harder than usual. It would be nice if this apartment had a full-length mirror so she could see if her shoes looked okay with the dress.

She'd better text Avery now.

More uneasiness nudged at her. But why? Avery was the one who had something to feel guilty about, not Lana.

Forgive.

The word popped into her head out of nowhere. Inadvertently, she glanced over at her Bible.

Forgive.

It was at the center of the New Testament.

But Avery was so…awful. In addition to embarrassing Lana, the woman was trying to ruin the boys ranch.

Lana leaned close to the small mirror, adding a little eyeliner and mascara. Light and natural, for church. Just an enhancement.

Just something Flint might notice and admire.

Except she couldn't meet her own eyes, and reluctantly, she finished up her makeup and sank back down into her chair.

If Avery was telling the truth, she'd been raised in foster care and hadn't had an easy time of it. That her pain came out in difficult behaviors shouldn't be a surprise. Lana saw it all the time in her first-graders. The kids who needed love the most acted the least loveble.

What had Avery said? Haven, Texas, was a hard place to move to from Dallas. And it would be, if you didn't know anyone.

Lana knew about loneliness. Maybe that

was why the Lord had put it on her heart to invite Avery to come to church.

She blew out a sigh. The Lord *had* put it on her heart. She needed to obey.

If nothing else, church would keep Avery out of trouble for a few hours. Lana didn't like the woman, and she didn't expect to enjoy their time together. But at least she could take the right action. Maybe a better attitude would follow.

Resigned now, Lana was just about to leave her pleasant armchair and finish getting ready when she sensed God keeping her anchored there.

What is it, Lord?

Forgive.

She didn't actually hear the word, but the idea of forgiveness filled her mind, and she propped her cheek on her hand, wondering. She'd decided to do the right thing by Avery, right? She was trying.

Forgive.

There was that idea, echoing again. So it

was something else, and reluctantly, Lana sank back into the chair and closed her eyes, Bible in hand.

Something fluttered out of her Bible. The prayer card one of her friends had given her after she'd been jilted at the altar.

She picked it up, blowing out a breath. *Really, Lord?*

She guessed it was time. Tentatively, cautiously, she let her feelings and thoughts turn to the second most difficult day in her life, just behind the loss of her parents.

Her supposed-to-be wedding day.

Did she have to go there?

Probably so.

She squeezed her eyes shut and hugged her knees to her chest and forced herself to think about that day. To remember standing in the back of the church among her three purple-clad bridesmaids, heart fluttering. To remember the warm spring air blowing through the open church door and the fragrance of her lilac bouquet.

Then, through the side door that led to the pastor's study, Gregory had approached with the pastor. He hadn't looked like a joyous groom. No, his face had been full of anguish and dread.

They'd pulled her into a small back parlor. And she'd known. Actually, the moment she'd seen them approaching, she'd known.

Hearing Gregory say the words, seeing the tears stream down his cheeks, feeling the pastor's hand patting her shoulder...each moment had sealed the lid on her romantic dreams of a happy, traditional married life.

Now, she forced herself to remember Gregory's words, to pay attention. He'd said he just wasn't ready, wasn't sure he even wanted to be married. That he'd let physical attraction push him toward something he now felt was wrong for him.

A couple of tears escaped as she felt the loss and humiliation all over again, but she brushed them away and forced herself to think about what he'd said, about the relationship they'd had. Now, with the benefit of hindsight, she realized she should have seen the signs. Unlike Gregory, she'd been more than ready for marriage, absolutely sure she was made for it. Possibly to the point where she'd seized on the first somewhat promising candidate and pushed him in a direction he wasn't ready to go.

She saw now that her own deep longing for a family had made her too hasty to encourage Gregory into a proposal and then a wedding. Yes, he'd been wrong to go along with it. A gentle fellow teacher, eager to please, he hadn't had the spark to stand up for himself until the reality of marriage was upon them.

Flint would never have done that.

Where in the world did that thought come from? But it was true; she knew the quiet cowboy would never go along with an idea he knew wasn't right. He could listen, and he was willing to change, as he'd begun to do in his treatment of Logan, but only when he fully believed it was the right thing to do.

He was too strong to be pushed around, and Lana, knowing she could be a little too enthusiastic and assertive at times, would be better suited to a man like that: a man who was able to be strong in return.

The canceled wedding wasn't entirely Gregory's fault. She needed to accept her share in the problem. She needed to forgive him for his lack of courage in waiting until the last minute to break it off.

Tears stung her eyes. *Lord, You're sure building humility in me, aren't You?*

But one thing at a time. She'd work on acting forgiving toward Avery, and maybe do some thinking about Gregory. She closed her eyes and let out a sigh. The truth was, being jilted had saved her from a marriage to someone who wasn't strong enough for her and wouldn't ultimately have made her happy.

Thank You, Father. She stood up, still pondering. She might not have her earthly parents, but she had an even better guide in her heavenly father.

She stretched, caught a glimpse of the clock, and rushed to her closet to find shoes and a necklace. She'd have to hustle to pick up Avery in time. But being with God in prayer was definitely more important than lingering over what shoes to wear to church.

Fifteen flurried minutes later, Lana approached the Blue Bonnet Inn. Just one street away from Haven's downtown, the large, stately bed-and-breakfast boasted true Southern hospitality. On another day, Lana would have lingered on the walkway, but today she was hurrying.

At peace, but hurrying.

She'd just raised her hand to open the screen door that led into the foyer when she heard Avery Culpepper's voice. "I know, can you believe it? But one of the locals invited me, and I couldn't think up an excuse on the spot."

Lana paused. Was Avery talking about church?

"No! You know me. I only worship one thing in this life—money."

Taking a step back, Lana swallowed. Now she knew for sure that Avery had been talking about church. And that Avery's heart was very, very hard.

Which made Lana very, very worried about the boys ranch's future.

You're sure about this, Lord? But Lana knew He was. Sometimes the least lovable need love the most, she reminded herself. She knocked on the door and then opened it. "Hey, Avery! Ready for church?"

It turned out that Avery had been, in a certain way, ready for church, Lana reflected as she exited the pew at the end of the service. The woman looked way dressier than most of the congregation in her heavy makeup, form-fitting dress and super-high heels, her blond hair big and curled and bouncing down her back. She'd spent most of the service texting on her cell phone, but now that it had ended, she looked up and narrowed her eyes, scanning the sanctuary.

It was almost as if she was looking for her next opportunity to stir up trouble. Lana could only hope that some of the pastor's message had gotten into Avery by osmosis.

"There's coffee and doughnuts out in the church hall," she forced herself to offer. "And a couple of adult Sunday school classes, too. Everyone's very friendly, and you would be welcome to attend either one."

Avery stood. "Thanks. I'll probably check one out."

"Great! I can't go, since I teach a kids' class, but—"

"Well, of course you do," Avery said in a decidedly hostile voice.

Lana blinked. "But we can meet up afterwards so I can drive you home," she said, making herself continue in an even tone.

Avery's eyes lit on Eduardo Gomez, the recently widowed father of one of the girls in Lana's class. "That's all right, I'll find my own way home," she said, tossing back her hair and heading toward Eduardo just as his daughter, Valentina, rushed up to cling to her father's leg.

Lana blew out a sigh. Eduardo was still grieving the loss of his wife, and so was Valentina. He was also a member of the Lone Star Cowboy League and quite wealthy.

She watched as Avery put a hand on Eduardo's arm and then squatted down to pinch Valentina's cheek.

"I suppose you thought that was your Christian duty, bringing her here, but I call her a viper." Marnie Binder appeared at Lana's side. "Look at her, flirting with poor Eduardo."

"I'm sure Eduardo can take care of himself, but I worry about Valentina. She's so needy right now."

"And what she doesn't need is a gold digger trying to get at her daddy's money."

Uncomfortable with the conversation as much as with the scene in front of her, Lana turned away. "I'm going to grab some coffee and round up my munchkins before they get too sugared up. They're already a little crazy with Christmas coming."

But when she reached the large open hallway where refreshments were served, she realized she was too late. Several of the kids who were in her class were running through the area, jostling adults and generally causing a ruckus.

Lana squatted down and intercepted the two boys nearest her. "Colby! Damon! Time for class. Walking feet, please."

Colby, a former ranch resident who now lived with his aunt in town, looked ashamed. "I'm sorry, Miss Alvarez. C'mon, Damon."

The other boy, who'd taken Colby's place when Colby left the ranch, frowned as if he was about to defy the order. But between Lana's stern look and Colby's tugging at his arm, he turned toward the classroom wing.

"Disaster averted," Pastor Andrew said at her elbow, chuckling. "Thanks, Lana—"

Behind them, a crash sounded. All the chattering voices went still.

Lana turned. What now?

Logan and six-year-old TJ Johnson, stood, eyes wide, staring at Fletcher Snowden Phillips. The blustery lawyer must have been knocked down, because he sat on the floor, legs sprawled, with coffee spilled down the front of his white shirt. His Stetson lay beside him, and his hair hung to one side, revealing his bald pate. His face was almost purple, his mouth open.

"Prepare for explosion," Pastor Andrew murmured at her side. "I'm going in." He headed toward the man.

"I'll have your hides, you little hooligans!" Fletcher yelled, jamming his Stetson back on his head.

Conversation burst out again as everyone tried to explain what had happened. Two members of the Lone Star Cowboy League pulled Fletcher to his feet, and Marnie Binder bustled over with a handful of napkins.

"Now, Fletcher," Lana heard Marnie say as she dabbed at his shirtfront. "Those boys meant no harm. They just happened to knock you off balance. Are you all right?"

"No, I'm not all right!" he roared. "This is an outrage. Those boys run roughshod over our community, and it's got to stop."

Logan and TJ were backing away, both looking like they were about to cry. They needed to be taught how to do what was right, so Lana stepped forward and knelt between them. "What do you say to Mr. Phillips, boys?"

Logan gulped. "I'm sorry for knocking you down."

"Me, too," TJ quavered.

"Sorry isn't good enough." Fletcher's voice wasn't quite as loud, but his face remained dangerously red. "Town meeting. Tomorrow night. The Boys Ranch has to go."

As more members of the League circled around Fletcher, obviously trying to calm him down, Lana looked for Flint but didn't see him. Well, he'd find out what had happened soon enough. And fortunately, dealing with Fletcher Snowden Phillips was not part of her job; her responsibility was the children. "Come on, boys. We have a lot of fun things to do in Sunday school."

After an hour on the phone trying to find a part for one of the old tractors, Flint headed back into the church. He went to services for Logan's sake—and because he knew he needed to give the Lord some chance to work in him—but he wasn't about to participate in a Sunday school class. That was a little too personal. He might be called upon to talk about his faith.

Besides, he was in a foul mood. He'd glanced through the window into the church lobby just in time to see Lana Alvarez and the preacher talking intently together. Then, they'd rushed off to do something.

Which was absolutely fine. A good reminder. Lana needed to be with someone closer to her age, a young man like the preacher who wasn't weighed down with responsibilities. And Flint needed to get back to his quiet, independent life and to keep Logan on the right track.

Speaking of which, he wasn't pleased that Logan had played a role in Fletcher Snowden Phillips getting knocked down. Several churchgoers had pounced on him, one after another, to tell him about his son's misbehavior. He'd scold Logan and have him write Fletcher a note to apologize. But kids were kids, and it definitely sounded like Fletcher had overreacted.

No big surprise there.

He heard the church bells strikc noon, which meant Sunday school should be over. As usual, he headed around the church to the back door rather than making his way through the crowd inside. He'd get to the classroom, collect Logan and head back to the ranch.

Once inside, though, he saw that it wasn't going to be that easy. A crowd of parents stood in the hallway, while others drifted into the unoccupied side of the large room. Obviously, Logan's class wasn't over yet.

He got there just in time to help push aside the heavy vinyl curtain that divided the classroom in two. So he caught the sweet scent of the gingerbread cookies one of the families had brought. And even in his antisocial mood, he couldn't help but smile when he saw the kids decked out in their cute Christmas outfits. He was grateful Logan had insisted on wearing the Christmas sweater Marnie Binder had knit for him. He fit right in.

Lana Alvarez rose gracefully from the low table where she'd been sitting on a child-sized chair. "I'm sorry we're running behind," she said to the assembled parents. "Do you mind waiting five or ten more minutes? We're just putting the finishing touches on our project for today, and then we need to pray."

Everyone assured her that it was fine—well, everyone but Flint, but she didn't seem to notice—and started gathering around the coffeepot in the empty side of the room. Lana turned back to the stack of colorful drawings and notes the children had been making. And then she snapped her fingers. "You know what? Logan, Allie, could you ask your dad and mom to come in here?"

Logan ran to get Flint, and another little girl ran toward a twentysomething woman with short blond hair. Flint found himself tugged into the classroom, toward a table seating about ten kids close to Logan's age. Tugged into close proximity with Lana Alvarez, neatly thwarted in his desire to escape entanglement.

"Children, who can explain where we're sending these letters, and why?" Lana asked.

"To the soldiers," one child said.

"To heroes," said another.

"They're sad because they can't come home for Christmas," Logan explained seriously.

"Yes! And, children, did you know we have

two soldiers right here?" Lana gestured toward him and the blonde woman. "They're called veterans because they aren't fighting anymore, but they're still heroes."

Flint kind of hated this type of thing, but he knew it was important for kids. He looked over at the blonde, wondering if she was one of the few vets who ate up this kind of attention. Her subtle wince made him smile. She must feel the same way he did.

The children's eyes were round.

"Do you have any questions for Mr. Rawlings or Mrs. Pfeifer?" Lana looked up at them apologetically. "I'm sorry, I don't know your correct rank and title."

Flint waved a dismissive hand at the same time the Pfeifer woman did.

"Did you have to go away from home at Christmas?" one of the kids asked.

The blonde nodded. "I was overseas at this time last year," she said, squatting down to put her arm around her daughter. "And I'm so happy to be home with my Allie this year."

"How about you, Flint?" Lana asked. She was looking at him with something like compassion in her eyes. "Did you ever spend a Christmas away when you were serving?"

Flint didn't have to think about it, because he remembered all too vividly. He'd been in his early twenties and homesick as the sky darkened on Christmas Eve, thinking about his brothers attending services together back in Colorado. He'd watched as one of his buddies approached a truck that had stopped at their checkpoint outside the base.

The truck had exploded before his eyes. He'd run in and dragged his buddy out, but the man's injuries were too severe. He'd died the next day. On Christmas. "Yeah," he said through a throat suddenly gone tight. "It's not much fun."

"But the soldiers will be happy when they get our letters, won't they?" Logan asked, looking worried.

Flint squatted down, put an arm around Logan, and looked at the notes spread out on the table before him. "To a hero" and "thank you" and "Jesus loves you," all copied out with various degrees of accuracy, all accompanied by pictures of Christmas trees and presents and Jesus in the manger.

He swallowed hard and pulled Logan a little closer. "Yeah. They'll be real happy."

Lana must have sensed his emotion, because she didn't ask any more questions. "Children," she said, "let's pray over the cards."

All the children obediently bowed their heads, and Lana led them in a short prayer asking for the soldiers to stay safe and to know they were loved, both by their countrymen and by Jesus.

Flint blew out a breath. He wasn't always good at teaching Logan values, he knew. He did his best, but one frazzled father couldn't do it alone. He was grateful for the church, and specifically for Lana's teaching.

At the same time, his feelings about the whole thing were mixed. Because how much of an influence did he want the tall brunette to have on his son? If she was Logan's teacher and his Sunday school teacher and his nanny, wasn't she getting to be way too important a part of Logan's life?

Especially since she seemed to have a thing for the pastor? The *young* pastor who might leave the region anytime, possibly taking Lana with him?

"Parents, you can come in and take a look and get your kids," Lana called to the group still by the curtain. "I'm sorry we went overtime."

The parents surged over, helping with jackets and admiring the kids' work.

Too surrounded to escape, Flint heard about how the class was focusing on the bigger meaning of Christmas, not just getting presents, but giving and sharing the love Jesus had brought into the world with his birth. Last week, they'd made ornaments for nursing home residents. Lana passed around photos that showed the elderly residents holding the ornaments and smiling. "Remember," she called after a couple of parents who were leaving, "canned goods next week."

The other veteran glanced over at him and offered a hand. "Della Pfeifer. Fourth Infantry Division out of Fort Hood. Lana and Allie and I are going out to brunch at Lila's Café," she added. "Would you and Logan like to come?"

"Can we, Dad?"

Flint tried to think of an excuse, but nothing came to mind. Besides, going out would mean he didn't have to cook.

And the fact that spending time with Lana made his heart beat a little faster would just have to get suppressed. He'd toughen up soon, get to where she meant nothing to him. Maybe it would help if they saw each other on bland social occasions like lunch with other church people.

"Sure," he said. "We can go."

Allie and her mom wanted to walk from the church to the restaurant, and Logan begged to walk with them. Lana joined, too, leaving Flint to drive over. He wanted a quick escape route, and he truly did need to get back to the ranch right after brunch.

When he arrived, though, Lana and Logan walked up alone.

"Allie threw up!" Logan yelled, running toward Flint.

Lana followed more slowly. "She must have eaten too many gingerbread cookies. She and her mom turned back. They're going home."

"She's okay? Do they need anything?"

"She says not. Apparently, Allie has a weak stomach."

"Oh." Flint rubbed the back of his neck. The last thing he and Logan needed was to have lunch in a cozy threesome with gorgeous Lana Alvarez.

They stood in front of the café, which was starting to bustle with the after-church crowd.

Okay, how do you get out of this without being a jerk?

Marnie Binder leaned out the door. "Quick, get in here! I saved you a table!"

Lana headed inside, and Logan followed her. After a second's hesitation, Flint did, too. If they were going to sit with Marnie, that was all right.

Except, when they got inside, Flint realized that she'd saved them a tiny table—a little space right by the window, with barely room for three chairs around it.

"I'll let you guys stay, since there's only room for three," Lana said quickly. She sounded almost as eager to get out of this awkward situation as Flint was, which irritated him for some reason.

"Oh, no, I'm going to sit over there with my sister and brother-in-law and the kids," Marnie said, pointing at the table in the center of the café. "I just figured I'd grab this table for the next friends who came in. Which is you!" She beamed at the three of them.

Logan pulled out the chair facing the street and sat down. "You sit here," he said to Lana, "and Dad, you sit here." He pushed them toward the chairs on either side of his.

At least they weren't next to each other. But the table was so small that they were practically knee to knee. Every time he moved, his legs brushed against Lana's.

Up close like this, in the morning light, he couldn't help but notice her smooth, tanned skin, bright eyes and long, dark hair that reached the middle of her back.

How had this happened? Flint had a definite feeling of being railroaded into this brunch. And Lana looked every bit as uncomfortable as he was.

When he glanced around the diner, he saw Marnie whispering to the woman next to her and nodding in their direction, a smile on her broad face.

So that explained it, or part of it at least. Marnie was still matchmaking, or trying to.

Too bad she hadn't matched Lana up with the preacher, like Lana preferred.

Despite the busy sidewalk in front of them

and Logan's chatter, Flint and Lana's silence felt awkward. They had a long wait for a server, who was clearly struggling with the crowd. They'd just ordered coffee for the adults and chocolate milk for Logan when the pastor came in.

An idea formed in Flint's mind, and before he could think, he acted on it. "Pastor Andrew," he called, gesturing the man over as he stood. "Come, sit here."

The young pastor approached their table readily enough. "Doesn't look like there's room—"

"It's all right. I have a lot to deal with at the ranch. Logan and I need to leave."

"Dad!" Logan's face screwed up. "I want to eat pancakes."

"I can bring him home," Lana said faintly. There was something in her voice, but Flint couldn't pause to analyze what. He was on a quest. A quest to turn tail and run away just as fast as he could run.

"That would be great," he said. He stopped

at the counter, left way too much money to pay for the small group's breakfast, and hurried out the door.

Chapter Seven

That night, Flint helped Logan pile his sleeping bag, backpack and duffel into the Delgados' SUV and made sure Logan was happily chattering with his friend Martin in the backseat. "Thanks for inviting him," he said to the doctor's wife.

"We're glad Logan and Martin are becoming friends," she said. "We'll make sure he gets on the school bus in the morning."

"Thanks." Flint watched them drive away. Logan had begged for this sleepover, and Flint was glad to encourage the friendship. But he didn't relish spending the evening alone. Alone, with his own guilt.

As he'd left Lila's Café after church, he'd glanced in the window and seen Lana's stricken face. Sure, Flint had ultimately done her a favor by giving her time with the young pastor, but he'd done it in a rude way.

Cowboy nudged at his hand, and Flint looked down distractedly at the dog. "What kind of idiot am I, anyway?"

Cowboy cocked his head and let out a quiet bark, for all the world as if he were listening.

Not only had Flint been rude, but he'd given his rival a golden opportunity to hang out with Lana. Of course, the pastor *wasn't* his rival, because Flint wasn't in the running for a relationship. Especially a relationship with a beautiful young woman who, like his ex-wife, was likely to get tired of Haven and leave any day now. Well, any month. He'd recognized enough character in Lana Alvarez that he didn't think she'd leave her students in the lurch the way Stacie had left Logan.

But the principle was the same. She was

too young and pretty to be stranded in a small town for any length of time. He needed to protect himself and Logan from the over-involvement that was starting to happen.

Funny thing, though. His actions this morning had felt less like protection and more like cowardice. And that didn't sit right with him.

"Come on, let's walk," he said to the dog, and they headed down the dirt road that led toward the main ranch buildings and the barn. You couldn't help admiring that sky, lingering blue in the background, clouds of pink or dark gray, depending on where the setting sun hit them, an orange glow on the horizon. It was enough to make a cowboy go poetic.

Maybe even enough to make him give a nod to the Creator.

Looking at beauty like this, a guy had to believe in an all-powerful God. Had to think, maybe, that God had a plan.

Maybe Stacie wouldn't have done a good

job with Logan. Maybe she'd have hurt him more than she would've helped him.

Flint was sure enough happier without her, and that thought surprised him.

But he *was* happier now, he realized. He was getting a little perspective, realizing that life went on, even after a heavy blow. Even with his problems, he was much more fortunate than some of the guys he'd served with, for example. He'd escaped the war without physical injury or emotional damage. And where was the justice in that? He'd been young and single, while some of his buddies who'd lost their lives had been married with young kids.

Cowboy spotted some little critter and raced off after it, yipping joyously.

Maybe Flint had been saved for a purpose. If so, most probably, that purpose was Logan. None of it made much sense, but as he watched the sky darken to violet, he figured that maybe, just maybe, God was the one who should figure it all out.

He kicked at a stone, watched it disappear into the gathering dusk. Thinking spiritual thoughts didn't change how he'd approach life. He still wouldn't have a relationship, wouldn't risk Logan's heart.

And who was he kidding? He had to admit that his own heart was softening a little, and softening in a particular direction it shouldn't, and he needed to protect that, as well. Couldn't let himself head toward love, because that was a trip to the dark place he'd been after his wife had left him alone with a newborn baby. Now, Logan was old enough to notice. And Flint had to take some care.

He looked up and saw the barn to his left, but his boots kept walking toward the main ranch house.

He'd been a jerk, and he needed to apologize.

Just as he was turning toward the main house's front porch, he noticed a light on in the storage barn. He'd better check, see what was going on. They hadn't had any instances of sabotage since the missing child saddles, but you couldn't be too careful.

Funny how he'd rather confront a thief than a certain tall, slender female.

But God had the last laugh. Because when he got to the barn and looked through the open door, there was Lana.

She was hauling a hay bale from one side of the makeshift stage to the other, or trying to, leaning her whole weight against it, then stopping to rest, looking frustrated. He walked inside. "That's way too big for one person to handle alone," he said, approached her and bent to nudge at the bale. "Where do you want it?"

"That wall." They pushed more until the bale was secure against the painted manger scene. Lana straightened, brushed back her hair...and turned away without thanking him.

That wasn't like her. "Hey, listen," he said, "I wanted to talk about this morning."

She walked away. "I don't," she threw back

over her shoulder. She went and knelt by a container of foam shapes that were to be made into the Wise Men's gifts. She started pulling them out of the crate, not looking at him.

"Look, that was rude of me to leave," he said. "I'm sorry."

"Yes, it was!" she burst out, looking up at him with eyes that sent out dark fire. "Why did you do that, Flint?"

He hadn't gotten so far in his mind as thinking of how to explain. "I, um, had a lot to do back here. But I shouldn't have—"

"You think I didn't have a lot to do?" She gestured around the barn. "You think I wanted to spend two hours having brunch, so that I'd have to stay up late to get my work done here?"

"But you'd been planning to go," he said, trying to get the discussion on to reasonable ground and away from the dangerous area of why he really had wanted to leave. "Whereas I got sucked in at the last minute."

"I would've left if I'd known you didn't want to be there. I would've left when Allie got sick. But I couldn't go, could I, because you'd dumped me. And dumped Logan on me. And dumped both of us on Pastor Andrew."

"I didn't mean to dump you," he floundered. "Lana, any man would love to have a meal with you."

"Anyone except you," she fumed. "And just because you paid for it doesn't mean I'm not mad."

Flint tried not to get distracted by how pretty she looked, her cheeks pink, her eyes dark. Even wearing a Christian rock band T-shirt and ragged denim shorts, she was stunning.

He was bungling this apology and making her madder. "I just meant to—"

"Just because people like Marnie Binder are pushing us together," she interrupted, "that doesn't mean I'm on that train, Flint! You embarrassed me in front of a whole restaurant full of people. Left me and Pastor Andrew to try to explain where you went when we really had no idea. And to do it without upsetting Logan."

"I'm sorry." His hand wanted to touch her, but she'd probably slap him if he did. "Lana, I'm really sorry I did that. It won't happen again."

He forced himself to turn around and walk out of the storage barn.

Fuming, Lana watched Flint walk out into the almost-dark evening. How dare he come in here and think he could set everything right by moving a hay bale? Why, he'd dumped her in front of a roomful of...

Suddenly she stopped, drew in a breath.

Oh.

So that was why she'd gotten so upset she'd had a hard time not crying.

This wasn't the first time she'd been dumped in front of a room full of people.

But of course, when she looked at it logically, the situation at brunch was totally different than her wedding disaster. Flint hadn't made any promise to be with her. He'd been pushed into it, as he said, not by her but by Allie's mom and Logan and Marnie Binder.

And hadn't she learned anything from her prayer time today? She wasn't called to judge; she was called to forgive.

She hurried to the barn door. "Hey, Flint!"

He stopped. Turned slowly.

Silhouetted against the dark gray sky, he looked like the hero of a thousand cowboy movies she'd watched with her family as a kid.

"Can you come back here a minute?" And then she realized that was too commanding, and she walked out to meet him, standing outside the barn.

"Listen, I'm sorry I got mad," she said quickly, not wanting to lose her resolve. "I tend to have a temper. I appreciate your apology, and of course, I forgive you." There. Her heart was already lighter, and when she saw Flint's slow smile, it got lighter still.

There was a rustling sound in the bushes over by the fence, and then something flew toward them, some kind of missile. Flint shoved her behind him and caught it midair.

He looked at it as Lana's heart pounded… partly from the scare, and partly from Flint's protectiveness and the feel of his hands on her arm. "What is it?" she asked.

"I'm not sure. Looks like something you'd shoot from a toy gun. Couldn't hurt you bad, but…here." He handed it to her. "I'm going to see if I can find the kid who shot it. They shouldn't be aiming at people."

Lana took the projectile and noticed something rubber banded around it. A note? She slid the rubber band off and unfolded the note, backing into the barn and flipping on a light to read it:

"Stay away from Flint Raling. He is not a god boyfriend. Please marry me. Love, Pastor Andrew."

The note was typed, but the two misspellings suggested to her that the true author wasn't a grown man who'd completed college and seminary. More like a second-or third-grader. What in the world?

"What is it?" Flint asked, coming back.

For some reason, she felt self-conscious as she showed him the note. It actually had the opposite effect from the sender's intention, in that it was actually making her think about Flint Rawlings as a boyfriend.

What would it be like to be the handsome cowboy's girlfriend? Feeling easy with him, getting together to talk of an evening, sliding an arm around that narrow waist?

The direction of her thoughts annoyed her. She was *not* going to think of Flint that way. He had too many issues, and so did she. "Just another silly note, like with the cross necklace last week. Somebody seems to be bent on matchmaking."

An expression of surprise crossed his face,

so fleeting that she wasn't sure she'd seen it. "That little present wasn't from the pastor?"

She shook her head. "The note was full of misspellings, just like this one. It's kids. But what I don't understand is why."

He nodded. "It's a puzzle. I think some other people in the community have been getting similar notes, right?"

"I guess." Obviously, the thought of being partnered with her hadn't flustered him the same way it had flustered her. She put her hands on her hips and surveyed the barn, trying to decide what to do next.

"So, what else needs to be done tonight?" He came up to stand beside her.

Her breath hitched. "That's what I'm trying to figure out. I'd like to have everything ready for tomorrow's rehearsal, which means having the stage set up for the first scene. And I need to have a table where the sets people can work on the movables. Gifts for the Wise Men, crooks for the shepherds, you know." As she spoke, she moved just a little bit away from him. There. That helped her calm down. She rubbed her hands together.

"Since I helped cause the backup, I ought to help you finish up." Without waiting for her to answer, he went over to a storage stall, slid out a long table, and picked it up easily. "Where do you want it?"

Man, those muscles! She swallowed. "Um, over there."

Once she got herself under control, she appreciated his help. He didn't talk much, but he was quick to see what was needed, and he did it. When she changed her mind about the placement of the cutout moon and stars, he climbed up to the loft and walked nimbly out on the exposed rafter to move them, making her gasp. They had a laugh over the rough job the younger boys had done at sanding the manger. And when the barn door opened wider and she stepped back into him, worried, he put an arm around her and whistled, and Cowboy came trotting up.

"Did you know it was him?"

He chuckled. "Heard him bump open the door with his head. I've heard that sound a thousand times." He gave her shoulders a quick squeeze and then let go, bending down to pat the dog who stared adoringly up at him.

She set him to work folding the lengths of cloth someone had donated, which would serve as costumes, and sorting them out by size, while she sat on a hay bale making a couple of last-minute changes to the stack of scripts. Even that domestic task he did willingly and well.

"Thanks!" she said in half an hour, looking around with surprise. "That would have taken me much longer by myself."

"More hands lighten the load." He grinned. "My mom's saying. Helped keep all of us brothers on task. Are we done here?"

"I think we are. Thank you."

They walked out of the barn together. And maybe it was the moonlight, or the fact that he'd helped her, or the quick touch of his hand at the small of her back, easing her out of the way so he could close and bolt the barn door. Whatever it was, it gave her a soft, romantic feeling right around the heart.

She watched him test the bolt's security. There wasn't an ounce of fanfare or showing off in the man. It couldn't be easy, being the foreman for a ranch, mentoring a bunch of boys with major challenges, and raising a son alone, but he did it without complaint and found time to help the community in a million small ways, too.

He just worked hard and did the right thing. Like apologizing when he was wrong; like offering a helping hand.

With a shock she realized she was coming to like and admire the taciturn cowboy. Not just to think he was attractive, but to actually like him.

Although, with his face ruggedly handsome, she had to admit he was a pleasure to look at, too.

He turned back toward her and caught her

staring. He took a step toward her, his head tilted a little to one side. "What?" The single word rumbled out, seeming to create a vibration in her own chest.

"Um, nothing." She shrugged, laughing nervously.

He took another step toward her, his eyes speculative. He reached out, put one hand on her shoulder. Then the other hand on her other shoulder. The solid weight of them warmed her, made her feel protected.

Although, when she looked up into his stormy eyes, she didn't feel exactly safe.

Flint Rawlings was kind and helpful. He could be gentle to kids and patient with a balky cow or an interfering acquaintance.

But he'd seen and done things she'd never even dreamed of. The tiny wrinkles beside his eyes, the scar that, she now saw, crossed his eyebrow and disappeared into his hairline, told her there was a lot she didn't know about the cowboy.

And it wasn't just general life experience.

It wasn't even just the fact that he'd been to war.

Flint Rawlings was almost ten years older than Lana was. More experienced in relationships, just like everything else.

Lana gulped in a breath, tasting the hay-scented air and shivering in the night breeze. Her eyes were locked on his. She couldn't have looked away if her life depended on it.

But her mind was racing. He was the parent of a child in her classroom. He was her boss. He was...well, he was Flint Rawlings, danger in a tall, rugged package. And she should turn around and run far, far away. Except that she really, really wanted to know what it would feel like to kiss him.

His two hands came closer together to rest on either side of her face. She could feel their roughness, their size. Now her breathing was rapid, as if she'd just run a race.

"Sssh," he said, his mouth quirking up the tiniest bit at one side. "It's okay. You're okay."

"Is it? Am I?" She tried to grasp at her

faith, at what God would want her to do, but the man in front of her wouldn't give her the distance she needed to refocus. Instead, he moved just an inch closer, his hands on her cheeks tightening just slightly.

She couldn't have moved if she'd wanted to.

The trouble was, she didn't want to.

"I'd sure like to kiss you right now." He let his thumb trace her lower lip, slow and lingering, bringing it alive with sensations she'd never felt before. Could he feel it trembling? Feel *her* trembling, or hear her heart racing?

She still couldn't look away as his hand moved to brush back her hair, as gently as you'd touch a sleeping baby.

Her lips parted a little. Nervously, she bit her bottom lip.

He closed his eyes for a moment. Opened them and looked off to one side. Took an audible breath, and stepped back, letting his hands fall from her shoulders. "But that wouldn't be the thing to do, would it?"

She was still staring at his face, now turned away from her, so she saw a muscle jump in his cheek.

"Go on inside," he said in a voice that was barely louder than a whisper.

"Flint…"

"Go on, now. Hurry. I'll watch to make sure you get there safely."

Something in his ragged tone scared her. She turned and ran toward the main ranch house as fast as if she were running from an oncoming train.

Flint watched her go, berating himself for being a fool. He'd just gotten back in her good graces, and now he'd insulted her again.

Whether by talking about kissing, letting her see how much he wanted to kiss her, or by not doing it, he wasn't sure which.

He just knew she'd looked more beautiful than any woman he'd ever seen. Her hair had felt as soft as a baby bird's feathers, and her lips…well. He'd wanted to pull her into his arms and never let go. Wanted to kiss away her worries and the loneliness that always seemed to hide just behind her smiling, helpful exterior.

And what a big mistake that would have been.

He'd gotten carried away when he'd learned that she didn't like the pastor, that the gift he'd assumed came from the other man was actually a poorly executed, juvenile attempt at matchmaking. So he'd been mistaken in thinking that she and the pastor wanted to be together. Figuring that out had made him feel like a weight had been lifted off his chest.

And then he'd discovered that they could work out a problem together. She'd been mad at him, but then she'd apologized and forgiven him. And she'd truly forgiven him; they weren't just words. She hadn't referred to his rudeness again but had joked with him in a totally comfortable way. She could both forgive *and* forget, it seemed. A rare quality in anyone, but especially in a woman.

She was the kind of woman a man wanted to kiss, sure. She was breathtakingly beautiful, with a warmth and spark that promised things every man wanted.

But she was also the kind of woman who would make a great wife. Giving, kind, motherly. Full of life and energy. Able to laugh and have fun, even when pushing bales of hay around a dusty stage.

He looked up at the sky, now bright with stars. How far away they'd always seemed. How far away God had seemed.

Now, he seemed to feel the Creator all around him. And some of that, some of his coming back to God, that was Lana, too.

There was an ache in his chest, like he was coming alive again. His whole body felt awake and eager.

Once, out hunting as a teenager, he'd seen a black bear emerging from hibernation after a long, cold Colorado winter. He'd watched, fascinated, as it had lumbered out of its den, stretched, shook itself, blinked at the winter sun on snow.

Eventually, it had meandered off into the woods, picking up speed, majestic and dangerous. Maybe it was just his boyish imagination, but the bear had seemed happy to be awake and moving on to its springtime life.

For just a minute there, he'd felt as if *he* was moving on to springtime and new life, like that big old bear.

Only they weren't animals, and life wasn't simple. There was a little boy he needed to look out for. And seeing the innocent longing in Lana's eyes, he realized there was a vulnerable woman he needed to look out for, too.

Maybe on a moonlit night at a lonely time of year, Lana Alvarez would have kissed him. Maybe she even thought she liked him a little.

But she was young and naive. She didn't know what she'd be getting herself into, connecting with Flint. He came with baggage.

He turned and walked back toward his empty cabin. Letting himself feel the pain of what he wanted and what he couldn't have.

Starting tomorrow, he was going to have to be more clear about that. To himself, to Lana, and to Logan.

But for tonight, he'd let himself think about what might have been.

Chapter Eight

The next evening, Lana wandered through the farm supply store in a happy haze. The place was crowded with people out to finish their errands before the town meeting that Fletcher Snowden Phillips had called for tonight. Despite the seriousness of the meeting, though, people were in a good mood. Christmas music played over the speakers, and one whole aisle of the store was dedicated to Christmas decorations.

Lana ran a hand over the old-fashioned boxes of tinsel. When she was a kid, she and her parents had decorated the tree together each year, tuning the radio to a Christmas station, drinking rich hot chocolate, and eating *buñuelos* as they'd filled their live tree with brightly colored lights and tinsel. As often as not, she'd catch her parents kissing under the mistletoe.

Although those memories were bitter-sweet, Lana was mostly seeing the sweet of it all today. For the first time, she was daring to hope that she might have family and a Christmas tradition of her own, drawing on what her parents had done, but also including her own creativity and whatever traditions her husband brought from his family.

And when had she started thinking about a husband as a possibility again?

But the truth was, she knew exactly when: it was that moment when Flint had gotten close to her, had said he wanted to kiss her.

The memory brought a smile to her face and a worried flutter of emotions to her heart. Maybe having a half hour to herself, wandering through the store, was not such a good thing.

"Hey, girl!" Someone tapped her on the shoulder, and she turned to see her friend Rhetta. "I've been calling your name for the last five minutes! What are you doing here?"

Lana blinked and then reached out to hug her friend. "I'm sorry. I guess I was daydreaming."

"You've been doing that all day. What's up with you?"

Lana shrugged, but she couldn't keep a smile from tugging at the corner of her mouth. "I just…had an interesting evening."

"Oh, girl, spill!" Rhetta glanced across the store. "I've got at least three minutes before the kiddos get restless and turn into monsters it takes two to handle." Rhetta waved her hand at the tall African-American man who was walking in their direction, twin three-year-olds tugging at each of his hands. "Go away, Deron, I've got girl talk to do."

Deron chuckled and veered off toward the aisle containing mysterious looking tools and parts. "I'll do what I can, for as long as I can," he tossed over his shoulder in his deep voice.

"So, what happened last night?" Rhetta tucked Lana's arm in hers and tugged her toward a display of tiny trucks and tractors.

"I...I don't know, exactly." Lana reached out and fingered the smallest of the toy vehicles. "I'm going to get enough of these for each of the boys in my class. Maybe for each of the girls, too. What do you think?"

"I think they'll love it. Don't change the subject."

"I don't have a subject. Nothing happened. I was just...working on the Christmas pageant, at the ranch, and...I got some company. That's all."

"Uh-huh. Was it a cowboy?" Rhetta murmured. "Who's a parent in your class?"

"Maybe." Lana couldn't keep the smile off her face.

"This is the most excited I've seen you since school started. Pay attention to that feeling, you hear?"

Lana shrugged. "I don't know where it's going, if anywhere."

"Yeah, but...that sparkle in your eye. It's how I felt when I met Deron."

"Did I hear my name?" and "Mama!" came from behind them, and Rhetta leaned back and picked up one of the twins. Deron swooped up the other and put his now-free arm around Rhetta, and Lana felt a sharp longing.

Would her time ever come? Could it be coming now? Could God have more for her than she'd ever dared to hope, not just a nice man, but a wonderful man with a wonderful little boy?

Rhetta cuddled her son close and gave Lana a friendly side hug. "Remember, pay attention to that feeling!" she whispered in Lana's ear.

Lana watched Rhetta, Deron and the boys head toward the checkout. Dreamily, she picked out small trucks and tractors for her students, dropping them into a red plastic shopping basket. She wanted to do just that. She wanted to let go, to listen to the romantic Christmas songs, and to dream she'd get love for Christmas.

But why had Flint backed off instead of kissing her? He'd definitely seemed interested. But then he'd sent her away, almost as if he felt it was dangerous for her to stay in his presence. She'd felt glad at the time, nervous as a schoolgirl, frightened of the intensity that rumbled in his voice at the same time that it thrilled her. But now she wondered, if he'd really wanted to kiss her, why hadn't he?

Goodness, she was acting just like a teenager. Like the teenager she'd never had the chance to be, because while other girls were giggling together about boys, Lana had been arranging a double funeral and then dealing with the house full of memories, the paperwork and the grief.

Oh, she'd had help. This community wouldn't let a young girl handle something so awful alone, and she'd been unofficially adopted by the parents of a school friend within weeks of her parents' death. In fact, the Waldrops still wrote from Louisiana where they'd moved, and they always invited her to their family holiday celebrations.

The truth was that even in her pain, she'd been blessed, and she sent up a quick "thank You" to the Father above, who'd seemed to draw her closer every year since she'd lost her earthly parents.

There were still twenty minutes until the meeting, so she wandered down the aisles of the feed store, checking out the stacks of poultry and pig feed, inhaling the scent of straw and sawdust, running a hand over the leather harnesses that reminded her of her preteen infatuation with all things horse-related.

When she heard Flint's voice, she felt at first that she'd imagined it. But, no, that was him for sure, talking to someone out in the main aisle.

Her heart gave a funny little flutter, and Rhetta's words echoed: *Pay attention to that feeling.*

Should she go over, talk to him? Would that be too forward?

She'd just resolved to speak to him when she registered what he was saying.

"I'm glad you're happy, man, but it's not for me. Logan's all the family I need."

Lana froze, her hand on a bag of beet shreds.

Another man's voice rumbled, and then she heard Flint again, loud and clear: "I tried marriage once. Not going there again."

Very slowly, Lana pulled her arms in and wrapped them around her stomach. *Stupid, stupid feelings.* Why had she let herself feel those feelings?

She'd opened herself up to dreaming about the future, dreaming she could have what Rhetta had, that she could be part of a family again. Most especially, that she could have a wonderful man to love, one who loved her back.

But of course, that wasn't meant to be. She'd known that, she'd resigned herself to it. She'd accepted the Lord's calling on her to be a teacher, not a wife and mother.

That fluttery feeling was just temporary, a silly, earthly thing for a silly woman who had romantic daydreams that couldn't come true. Why hadn't she remembered that her daydreams couldn't come true? You'd think getting jilted in front of a whole church full of people would be enough of a lesson.

Her eyes burned with tears, ridiculous tears she had no right to shed. Flint hadn't led her to believe their relationship could be anything but professional. When it had tilted otherwise, he'd wisely and kindly backed away, sent *her* away.

There was no reason for her to blame anyone but herself.

She drew in a breath and blinked and turned around. She'd take the side aisle up to the counter, pay for her things, and sit in her car until the meeting, pull herself together. If she had to have a good cry—and sometimes, you just had to—she'd do it in privacy.

She turned the corner, head down. And ran right into something.

Someone.

"Lana!" Flint's arms were on hers, steadying her. "What are you doing here?"

She cleared her throat and blinked and swallowed, her face heating. "Shopping for the kids," she managed to get out, nodding down toward her basket full of toys. She stepped back and he let go.

She couldn't look into his eyes. No matter what *wasn't* between them, she was afraid of what he'd recognize. In just a short while, he'd managed to get to know her better than most people did, and she was afraid of what he would see.

"Well, looky there." It was Heath Grayson. One of Flint's good friends, the one he must have been talking to, explaining how he didn't want to get married. Because Heath was marrying soon, he must have been urging Flint to consider the same path. "How are you doing, Lana? What've you got there?"

"Are those for the children in your class?" It was Josie, Heath's girlfriend, carrying a couple of bottles of liniment and a bag of medicated poultry feed. "You're the best teacher, Lana. Everybody talks about what a great job you're doing with the first-graders."

"Thanks," Lana murmured, and took a deep breath. Then another.

She could do this. She could talk normally to her friends. She could go up to the register, pay for the items, take them to her car.

If she could get that far, then she'd see about whether she could handle the town meeting.

Josie patted her baby bump. "I hope when this one gets to first grade, you're still teaching here."

What did it matter whether she stayed or went? She was totally without ties. Nothing was holding her to Haven, nothing except some nostalgic memories. And nothing was calling her anywhere else, either.

"Are you okay?" Flint asked.

She glanced up to find his blue eyes studying her. She swallowed. "I'm fine. Just a little tired."

"I'm guessing those first-graders are crazy this time of year," Heath said. "Tell you what, I'd rather break a wild colt than face a first-grade class every day."

"I'm going to have to face them later this week," Flint said. "Helping with the party."

Oh, right. She couldn't escape Flint even at work, because he was going to come to class. She drew in a deep breath and let it out in a sigh.

"You're helping with a Christmas party for kids?" Heath snorted. "Wish I could be a fly on the wall."

"Hey, Flint's a good dad," Josie protested. "He'll do fine."

Lana listened while the ribbing went on,

noticed with one part of her brain that Flint handled it well and was able to laugh about himself. Just another thing to like about him.

He was cheerful and understandably so. He'd done the right thing when his son's nanny and teacher had gotten a little too close in the moonlight. He'd pushed her away.

He knew who he was and what he wanted. He'd made decisions about his life, and he was obviously comfortable with them.

She was the one who was messed up, listening to her own traitorous feelings. Listening to her own hunger for a family. Not learning from experience.

"I need to go get this stuff paid for," she said, interrupting the others. A little awkward, but that was better than bursting into tears in the middle of the feed store. "Nice to see you guys." And she hurried up toward the cash register.

Once she'd paid, she walked out of the store into a wonderland. Darkness had fallen, and the streets were wet from a light rain. It was the first time she'd been downtown since they'd put up the Christmas lights.

Every tree, spaced at even intervals along Main Avenue, was wrapped in white twinkle lights, which extended up into the branches. Most of the shops had their windows lit with Christmas displays.

Lana drew in deep breaths of the warm, damp air as she headed to her car. She put her things inside.

She loved the town of Haven. Loved her job here, loved living here so much more than she'd liked living in a big city, during and after college. When she got job notices from big-city school districts—as happened fairly often—she threw them right into the trash.

Yes, she'd gotten her hopes up and her feelings hurt. But the best solution for hurting was to keep busy.

She climbed into her car and headed for the meeting at the church.

* * *

Ten minutes after leaving the feed store, Flint approached the church where the meeting was being held. Wreaths decorated the doors, lit by spotlights, and Christmas lights wrapped the bushes and railings outside the church.

"Colored Christmas lights," Flint said aloud.

"They're the best!" a woman he knew vaguely agreed, climbing the steps behind him. "Hate the white ones."

"*I* think white is classy."

"No way!"

Flint chuckled as he held the door for the others to enter. During his short marriage, one of the many arguments he'd had with his wife was over Christmas lights. She'd liked classy white ones, while he had grown up with the multicolored ones.

He'd given in, and willingly. He wasn't one to sweat the small stuff. But like with so many of their arguments, it had turned into a question of Flint's taste and background and general character.

Now, on his own, he'd made sure that Logan knew colored lights were the manly way to go.

Shaking his head at himself, Flint trotted down the stairs into the church basement where the meeting was being held. The room was packed with far more people than usually attended. That probably meant Fletcher had been out politicking. Fortunately, the LSCL had done their part to make sure advocates of the ranch attended the meeting.

Many of the attendees wore colorful sweaters, Christmas jewelry or bright holiday ties. What they lacked in snow, his fellow Texans made up for by going all out on decorations and Christmas clothing. Around the borders of the room, long tables stood with items for sale from the church bazaar. Trust Marnie Binder to take advantage of an opportunity to drum up more interest in the church's wares.

Fletcher Snowden Phillips wasn't dressed in red. He wore his usual dark suit and bolo tie, and he was holding forth to a circle of townspeople, waving his hands.

Where was Avery Culpepper? She surely wouldn't miss an event so possibly detrimental to the ranch. Flint scanned the room and saw her talking with a rancher Flint knew a little, Eduardo Gomez. The man, a recent widow, was rubbing the back of his neck and looking around. Searching for an escape route he wasn't going to find, because Avery was standing very close to him and had a hand on his arm. Poor Eduardo.

The meeting hadn't started yet, and the loud voices and gossiping clusters of people gave Flint a headache. He stuck to the perimeters of the room, pretending interest in the knitted toilet paper holders and wooden Christmas ornaments.

When he saw the sign beside a stack of Popsicle-stick picture frames, he paused. "Made by Miss Alvarez's Class."

He'd buy Logan's, he decided. Surprise the boy with a photo of the two of them or of Cowboy, in a frame Logan had made himself.

He flipped through the frames, looking for Logan's and marveling at the painstaking work. How had Lana gotten a bunch of first- and second-graders to sit still long enough to do this, on top of making cards for veterans and who knew what else?

She gave too much. She was running herself ragged. Maybe that was why she'd looked so upset over at the feed store. Almost like she was ready to cry.

She should take a break. As the employer for one of her jobs, he should give her a break. Offer her a leave from nannying, at least until school was out.

Elsa Wells, the town mayor, called the meeting to order. But before she could start with old business, Marnie Binder stood up and reminded everyone to check out the offerings from the Christmas bazaar. "It's this

Saturday, and what's left will be available after church, but don't wait until then," she said.

"Let's get to the point of the meeting." Fletcher Snowden Phillips stood and headed for the front of the room. "We've all put up with the Boys Ranch for long enough."

"Now, hold off, Fletcher." Elsa quelled him and forced the meeting to proceed in the proper order, dealing with old business first. But since there was only one real topic, soon enough Fletcher was back at the center of things. "The Boys Ranch scares off potential developers and home buyers. All those troubled hooligans running around our homes and our church, causing trouble. It's got to stop. For the sake of the town, it's got to stop!"

"Sure you're not just upset about being knocked on your hind end yesterday, Fletcher?" As a few titters spread through the room, Marnie stood, hands on hips. "It may have made you look a little silly, but it wasn't the fault of the Boys Ranch."

"I could have been seriously hurt!" Fletcher sputtered, his face turning red.

Flint stood, cleared his throat and waited until he had everyone's attention. "I'd like to point out that the church incident wasn't just Boys Ranch kids. My Logan was at least half of the problem. I should have been paying more attention, and I apologize again for that, Fletcher. But the point is, that incident was just kids being kids. It was nothing to do with the Boys Ranch."

As he sat down amid nods and "that's rights" he noticed Lana watching him. But when she saw him notice her, her face closed, and she turned away.

"It's not just the assault on me," Fletcher roared. "There's been graffiti marring our beautiful buildings and ranches. A series of thefts. The place is a menace, and I want it closed down. Who's with me?"

A few people murmured assent, and that was enough for Fletcher. "I call for a vote!"

"Now just a minute." A voice from the back of the room had everyone turning their heads. Nick McGarrett, a former soldier who volunteered at the ranch, was standing up. "My ranch was one of the places that got hit, but I don't believe the boys did it. As a matter of fact, the Boys Ranch has done this community a lot of good. Helps kids whose families can't set them right."

As Nick went on offering a rousing defense of the ranch, Flint relaxed. Fletcher wasn't going to win the day as long as well-respected people like Nick were offering testimonials. Or at least, Fletcher's win wasn't assured.

His mind drifted a little. Why had Lana looked away as soon as she'd seen him watching her? Why had she behaved so oddly at the feed store? Was it the fact that he'd come so close to kissing her? Was she offended, angry with him?

Thinking back over last night swept Flint's attention right out of the crowded meeting room and back to the starry night. She'd looked so pretty. And when he'd run a hand over that silky hair, when he'd touched her face, he'd felt her trembling. And not entirely with fear. She felt something for him.

Lana was a special lady, that was for sure. Unbelievable that someone had left her at the altar. Whoever ended up marrying her would be blessed.

And he didn't need to be thinking about that. He shook his head and forced his attention back to the meeting room.

Nick was still talking, but Flint got distracted by some overpowering perfume. Who would wear that much perfume? He glanced behind him. Of course. Avery Culpepper.

Lana wouldn't wear perfume like that. Her hair smelled simple and sweet, like wild honeysuckle.

Flint reined in his emotions. He had to remember what he'd been talking to Heath about. His resolve to be single. He shouldn't be making himself miserable thinking about something—or someone—he couldn't have.

The response to Nick's speech was much bigger than the response to Fletcher's had been; a few of the women were wiping tears. Flint resolved to congratulate Nick, who generally kept to himself. The man had made a difference, maybe even turned the meeting around.

"Folks, we've heard the two different sides of the issue, and that's a good thing. Open communication, not tale-bearing—" Elsa looked severely at a few known gossips in the room "—that's the key to a healthy community. However..." She stopped to makes sure she had everyone's attention. "The truth is, Fletcher, the location of the Boys Ranch in Haven isn't up for a vote."

The crowd started murmuring. "That's right, not a city entity," someone said nearby.

"We'll see about that!" Fletcher yelled.

"There are other ways to bring that place down!" Jamming his Stetson on his head, he stormed out.

The room burst out with excited chattering, and Elsa had to pound on the podium to get people's attention. "This meeting is adjourned," she called, and the room broke up into clusters of people talking it over.

Although happy with the outcome of the meeting, Flint knew that angering a man with Fletcher's power and influence wasn't wise. He knew he should talk to the other members of the LSCL about it, and he would. But first, he wanted to get to Lana, see if he could find out what was wrong and maybe repair any damages he'd done, offer to give her a break.

"Hey, Flint!" Someone tapped his arm, and Flint turned to see Gabriel Everett, president of the Lone Star Cowboy League. "What did you think?"

"I think we need to call a meeting of The League and figure out how to do damage control," Flint said, reluctantly pulling his attention away from his search.

Gabe nodded. "That was my take, too. Phillips isn't going to let this slide. This meeting just puts the ranch more at risk." His voice was rough with emotion, and understandably so; he'd spent a couple of years at the ranch as a boy, and he credited it with changing his life, putting him on the right path.

Flint scanned the room, still buzzing with clusters of townspeople. "All the more reason for us to double down on finding the original residents. Any progress?"

"Not on my end, and it worries me." Gabe's grandfather had been a resident of the ranch, but he'd disappeared when Gabe was eight.

"How are you going to punt?"

"Hired a PI, but so far nothing."

"Keep at it. Let me know if I can help." Flint clapped Gabe on the shoulder and watched as the man strode across the room.

But there was a bigger concern on Flint's mind, bigger even than the terms of Cyrus Culpepper's will, and that was a certain weary-looking schoolteacher. He'd offer to drive her back to the ranch, send someone for her car tomorrow. The woman needed a break.

Once again, unbidden, the memory of the soft skin of her face, the darkness of her eyes, the sound of her breathing, surged up inside him.

He checked the room once more and then strode out into the hall. No one. Looked into the church kitchen, where he could hear Marnie Binder's voice.

Lana wasn't there. She must have slipped out.

He headed out of the church building, picking up his pace. He'd seen her car in the parking lot. Maybe he could catch her in time.

As he rounded the corner of the church, he saw several cars pulling out of the parking lot.

Lana's was one of them, but even as he waved to stop her, her car's taillights shrank into the distance. He'd missed her.

Which shouldn't bother a die-hard single cowboy near as much as it did.

Chapter Nine

The next afternoon, Lana pulled her coat tighter as she and Logan walked out toward the ranch gates. As long as she stayed focused on the task at hand, she was doing all right. Fine. Better than fine.

"This is heavy!" Logan complained, stopping to shift the wreath he was carrying from one arm to the other.

"Here. I can carry it." Even though she was struggling with the other wreath, a big thermos of hot chocolate and some cups, she managed to thread Logan's wreath onto her arm. "You zip your coat up tight. And put your cap back on!" She made her voice stern.

"Okay." He pulled his warm hat down over his ears, and Lana couldn't help smiling. He looked so cute in winter clothes. It was the first time they'd really had cause to wear hats and mittens, and Logan looked downright Christmassy.

"Let me help with that, Miss Alvarez!" Robby Gonzalez came jogging up alongside them. He took the two wreaths from her arm and fell into step beside them. "What are you doing?"

"We're going to decorate the ranch gates. Want to join us?"

"I still get to hold the wreaths in just the right place, though?" Logan looked up at her anxiously.

She smiled down at him. "Of course you do. But Robby might be able to help with pounding the nails, because he's old enough to use a hammer."

"You hold, I'll hammer." Robby ruffled Logan's hair, and Lana smiled. She liked

Robby, and liked the way the older boys helped out the younger ones at the ranch.

As they walked, Lana tried to focus on the positive. She'd spent time praying and reading her Bible last night, and it had helped her a lot. She'd read the passages from Corinthians about marrying and staying single, and the wise words had shored up her resolve and her understanding.

There was nothing wrong with getting married, but if you *could* be single, that was the better route. You could focus on the work God wanted you to do.

If it was hard for you to withstand temptation, you should marry.

Lana had sighed over that part. Saint Paul seemed to be talking about physical temptation, but the Bible's meaning went beyond the surface. Her own temptation was wanting to belong to a family. Wanting it so badly that it sometimes overrode her better judgment.

Although, honestly, the physical temptation was there, too. Thinking about how Flint Rawlings had looked, standing up to Fletcher in the meeting, she felt her heart beat a little faster. There was no question that he was an attractive man. Not just in how he looked, but in his sense of authority. He knew what was right, and he didn't mind standing up to anyone who threatened those he cared about.

They reached the gates and put down their supplies. Cowboy bounded over, greeted Logan with a few well-placed licks, and then leaned against Lana's side. She reached down to pet the dog as they discussed the exact, perfect location for the wreaths.

Even though she was freezing, Lana let the boys take their time. Most of the boys on the ranch hadn't had the opportunity for shared family traditions, so Bea encouraged all the staff and volunteers to fill in those gaps whenever they could. She was sure that was why Marnie Binder had insisted on preparing a thermos of hot chocolate for their little decorating excursion. She was making it into an event, making a memory. While the boys argued, Lana busied herself with pouring small cups for each of them.

"Got enough for one more?"

The deep voice behind her made Lana slosh a little hot chocolate onto the ground. Flint. She hadn't seen him since the meeting last night, and that was on purpose. She'd left the church quickly and avoided him today.

She had to discipline herself. She'd gotten too attached, and she had to start keeping things more businesslike between them. Soon enough, Christmas would be over, and Flint would find another nanny, and she'd move back to her apartment in town.

The thought filled her with gloom.

"Hey, if there's not enough, I understand."

"There's plenty," she said woodenly, offering him a cup. The boys took their cups, too, tasting the hot beverage and experimenting with blowing out clouds of fog.

"Hey, I wanted to make a suggestion," Flint said. He took a sip of his hot chocolate and then turned toward Lana. "I wanted to offer you a break from being Logan's nanny."

Pain took Lana's breath away, rendering her unable to speak.

Logan didn't have any such problem. "No way!" he shouted. "I want Miss Alvarez to stay!"

"Well, but, buddy, she's overworking herself—"

"I'm not having Mrs. Toler again!" Logan yelled, hurling his hot chocolate against the white ranch fence and then throwing himself down on the ground, crying loudly.

Whoa. Lana blew out a breath, pushed aside her own upset feelings and knelt beside the boy. "Take some breaths, Logan," she said, putting a soothing hand on his arm. "Remember, we use our words."

"Hey." Flint knelt on Logan's other side. "Hey. Shape up."

Lana frowned at Flint. He didn't need to be stern when his son was that upset. But, surprisingly, it worked. A little. Logan's yelling quieted to softer fussing and gasping.

Cowboy pushed his way past Lana and nuzzled Logan's wet face. The boy's arm came out to wrap around the dog's furry body.

"Can you tell us what made you so upset?" Lana asked.

"I don't want you to go," he got out between sobs.

She patted his shoulder. "I feel the same way, buddy."

"Yo, Logan." Robby was holding the hammer and a wreath. "You want to try pounding the nail? Come on, I'll help you."

Logan sat up and looked over Robby's way.

"Go on, son," Flint said. "Miss Alvarez and I need to talk a minute."

Lana smiled thanks at Robby, as did Flint.

Flint, who wanted her to leave.

The moment Logan was focused on helping Robby, Lana turned back to Flint. "Not such a good idea to spring that on me and Logan at once."

"I'm sorry. I didn't realize it would upset him."

She just raised an eyebrow at him. Really?

"That was my mistake, and I apologize."

What could you say when a man offered an immediate apology? "Okay. But why do you want me to leave? Do you think I'm not doing a good enough job?"

"No, it's not that, not at all. I just...well, I saw how tired you looked last night, and I realized we were overworking you."

Lana felt her face get hot. So he'd noticed she wasn't herself. And was he really wanting to help her, or was that a convenient excuse to get rid of her? Her throat tightened, and she couldn't say a word, even though Flint was looking at her expectantly.

When she didn't speak, understanding dawned across his face. "Hey, I hurt your feelings. That was the last thing I meant to do."

Logan came back over and grabbed Lana around the legs. "Don't go, Miss Alvarez, please?"

Lana looked down at the little boy who was becoming dearer and dearer to her, and her throat constricted tighter. Tears burned at her eyes.

"Robby." Flint beckoned the other boy over. "Can you and Logan take this thermos back to the kitchen? I think Mrs. Binder just made some sugar cookies, and if you'll do this favor I'm guessing she'll give you some."

"Sure, no problem." Robby reached down for Logan's hand. "Come on, buddy."

"I want to stay and make sure—"

"We'll just go for a little while. I'll race you."

Logan looked tempted. Then he glared at his father. "If you make her go away, I'm not gonna like it."

"Logan. Adults make the decisions."

"But they listen to everyone before they decide," Lana interjected. She squatted down and put her hands on Logan's shoulder. "I promise I won't go anywhere without talking to you about it first, okay? And your dad will listen to your side of things, too. Right?" She looked up at Flint, her eyes narrowing, daring him to correct her.

His jaw squared like he didn't like her interference, but she just kept glaring at him. She might be bad at relationships, not a real candidate for a long-term one, but she definitely knew kids. And Logan had issues with women leaving him.

Finally, Flint nodded and squatted in front of Logan, too. "That's right, buddy. I'll hear your side before I decide."

"Come on, I'm gonna beat you!" Robby took off at a slow pace, carrying the thermos.

"No, you won't!" And Logan ran after the older boy.

Now alone, Flint and Lana watched them go. "Robby's a great kid," Flint said.

"And so is Logan. He needs to know he won't be suddenly abandoned."

Flint stared at her. "You think it's about his mother?"

"He's at an age where he's starting to understand he was left behind. Even though he didn't know her, he knows what a mother is, and it's got to hurt that his own mom left him."

Flint shook his head, leaning against the fence. "Wow. I never would have thought of that, but it makes sense."

"I know." But Lana wasn't going to get sidetracked. Now that she'd stuffed down her hurt, she was hopping mad. "Flint, what's wrong with how I'm taking care of Logan? Don't I even get a warning before you fire me?"

"I'm not firing you! Where did you get that idea?"

"When you tell someone you won't be needing their services anymore—even though the job hasn't gone away—that's what most of the world calls firing."

"You're totally misinterpreting what I said. I told you, you looked tired and overworked."

"So I have a few circles under my eyes the week before Christmas break. Try finding a teacher who doesn't." Even as she fumed at him, Lana knew she was being a little bit unreasonable. But she couldn't seem to stop herself.

Flint raised his hands to shoulder level, palms toward her. "Hey, okay. I'd rather have you continue. I'm just trying to do the right thing."

"You…what?"

"Actually, I don't know what we'd do without you." Flint picked up the wreath that hadn't been put up yet and pulled a nail from the little bag she'd brought.

"Really?" Relief washed over her at the thought that she didn't have to leave.

"Yeah, really." He put his supplies into one large hand and briefly cupped her cheek with the other, looking into her eyes for the fleetest moment.

He turned away so fast that she wondered

if she'd dreamed his touch. "I mean," he said, "look what you just did. You had insight into why Logan had a tantrum. I would've just yelled at him. Probably put him on the therapist's couch in later years, not that it's the first time." Flint held the wreath up to the gate post and studied it. "You're really good for him."

Seeing that he meant it, hearing the approval in his tone, made Lana feel warm, despite the winter chill. She felt the strongest urge to curl up in his arms.

"Does this look even?" he asked gruffly.

She stepped back and studied it. "Up about an inch."

He moved the wreath. "Now?"

"Perfect."

He pounded the nail, hung the wreath on it, and stepped back to study the entryway. "Looks good. Thanks for letting Logan decorate. He hasn't had much chance to get involved with Christmas traditions. I'm always so busy."

She nodded. "It's all good. I miss having

family to do stuff like this with." As soon as the words were out, she could have bitten her tongue. Logan wasn't her family, and neither was Robby Gonzalez.

Let alone Flint, who was looking at her with compassion in his eyes.

She must not let that happen, she reminded herself. She must not get closer to this family. She had to remember that she was the temporary nanny.

Her strong emotions at the thought of leaving were God's way of warning her.

"Lana, I—"

She held up a hand to prevent Flint's saying more. She'd keep things businesslike, and that would be best. "We'd better head back to the house," she said. "But as long as we have a minute, there's something I'd like to discuss with you."

Flint fell into step beside Lana, glad she wasn't mad at him anymore.

He wasn't even dreading whatever she

wanted to discuss, as he'd used to when his wife had done the "we need to talk" thing.

Maybe that was because Lana was so much better at expressing her feelings, clearing the air, and then letting it go. Or maybe a little bit of God's grace was seeping back in.

Whatever the reason, Flint wanted to stay close, work out any conflict, heal it.

Not that there was any comparison with a marital relationship here. He'd meant what he'd said to Heath in the feed store the other night. He didn't want to put Logan's heart at risk by starting something up with a woman. Women left.

And just because the pretty woman beside him was testing that resolve, that didn't mean he'd give in. Tests happened all the time, and the measure of a man was whether he could stand strong.

"So, about Avery."

"What?" Flint blinked.

"Avery Culpepper. I've been doing a little

digging, and…" She trailed off, drawing in a breath.

"Why were you digging? What about?"

"It's her coloring. She doesn't match the rest of the Culpeppers, from what I remember and from the pictures I've seen."

Flint cocked his head to one side, considering. "I knew Cyrus a little, but he was your typical old rancher. Skin like leather, white hair. You couldn't really guess his original coloring."

"But there's a picture in the school library. It's him and his family in younger days, and they're all brunettes. Kind of olive complexions. Anyway, I talked to a teacher I know in Dallas, and she made a couple of calls and dug up someone who thinks she had Avery in elementary school. If it's the same person, she had both her parents. But wasn't our Avery supposed to be an orphan?"

Flint's eyebrows rose as the implications of Lana's words sank in. "You think she's an impostor?"

"I hate to think anyone would do something so awful. She's probably legit. Except...she's not very interested in following Cyrus's wishes. She could have read the obituary and researched the Culpepper family after Macy left the message, and decided to impersonate Avery to get the inheritance."

Flint whistled as the concept took hold of him. "Only now she's mad because the inheritance turned out to be an old run-down cabin. So she's upping her game."

Lana put a hand on his arm and then just as quickly pulled it away. "It's possible, but, Flint, we can't make any accusations until we find out more. If Avery *is* who she says she is, imagine how horrible it would be to find out people thought you were a fraud."

"You're being too nice." Flint's mind was racing. If Avery wasn't Cyrus's daughter, then one of the threats against the boys ranch would be removed.

"No, I'm being a good researcher. Don't go

telling people about this yet, not until I have time to do some more digging."

Despite feeling like he should take over, being a member of the League and a guy, Flint had to acknowledge that Lana probably would be better at finding out more. "Okay, but we were just talking about how busy you are. Is this something you can take on?"

"Nothing's going to happen with the will over the holidays, is it? And really, once school's out and the pageant is over, I'll have more time."

That brought to mind the fact that Lana wouldn't be his employee forever, that she'd move back to her apartment in town at some point. That she'd eventually leave.

They were approaching the main ranch house now, and Logan exploded out the door and ran headlong to them, stopping himself by grabbing Flint's legs. "Can she stay, Dad?"

He looked down at Logan. "Yes, she's staying on as your nanny, though remember, it's only temporary." The warning was probably as much for himself as for Logan.

"Yes!" Logan pumped his fist in the air. "And can she stay and decorate the cabin tonight?"

Flint turned to face Lana. "Any idea what he's talking about?"

"Oh, we'd talked about putting up a few decorations. On the porch, and in the house."

Flint hadn't ever done much decorating for Christmas, relying on his connection to the ranch to give Logan a taste of the Christmas pretties. But he supposed Logan was getting old enough to want his own house decorated.

"Please? She said she would. And I looked at the clock, and it's not time for her to go home yet." He frowned. "The little hand wasn't on the five yet. It was in between the four and the five."

"You're right!" Lana squatted down and hugged Logan. "You're a very smart young man."

Flint was still trying to process the thought

of decorating his home with Lana Alvarez, and apparently, he'd missed something significant. "What did he just do?"

"He's *way* ahead of the curve on learning to tell time." Lana stood, her cheeks flushed and her eyes warm, and for a minute, Flint couldn't take his eyes off her.

Yes, she was pretty. Beautiful, even. But even more than her appearance, Flint admired her heart. Who got that excited over a learning milestone of a kid who wasn't even her own?

He tried to refocus on the question at hand. Out of habit, when making a decision, he looked around to assess the weather. Low, heavy clouds in a darkening sky, but it wasn't like Lana had to drive anywhere. None of them did.

"Can she stay, Dad, please?"

They were next to the ranch house now, but Flint kept looking upward. *Is it wrong, God, to have her stay when both of us Rawlingses want her to?*

He didn't get an answer, exactly, but he felt peace. "Would you stay?"

She bit her lip, thought for a minute, and then flashed a smile at him. "All right. Just let's grab Logan's and my stuff from the house."

So he and Logan followed her inside. When she handed Logan his backpack and got her purse out of the cupboard, an envelope fluttered to the floor.

Flint picked it up and handed it to her. Not before seeing what was written on the outside: *To Miss Alvarez from Mr. Denton.*

She studied it for a couple of seconds, her face blank. Then it cleared. "Mr. Denton. The mechanic who worked on my car." She ripped it open and scanned it, and then laughed outright. She handed the typewritten letter to Flint. "This is the first marriage proposal I've ever received by letter!"

Flint read it aloud: "'Please do me the grate honor of marrying me. I will never leave

Haven. My shop is called Denton and sons. We coud have some sons.'"

"It's pretty dircct," Lana said, still laughing. "I wonder who wrote it?"

"Mr. Denton did," Logan said, looking confused. "Right?"

Lana put a hand on his head. "Mr. Denton didn't write this, honey. That's not how grown-ups do things. Besides, I hardly know him, and he doesn't really know me, either."

Logan nodded, looking thoughtful.

Flint handed the note back to Lana. "We might want to give these to Bea. I've heard a few similar stories."

"She's probably in her office."

But when they showed the note to Bea, she frowned as she studied it. "The style of writing isn't the same as the other notes I've seen. Much younger. I wonder if we have some copycat matchmakers on our hands?"

"No harm done." Flint and Lana said the same words at the same time, then looked at each other.

Lana laughed.

Flint smiled.

Yes, they were on the same page again.

They chatted with Bea for a few more minutes and then headed out. Flint held the door for Logan and Lana to exit the ranch house ahead of him.

They both squealed at the same time.

"You okay?" Flint pulled the door closed and walked down the steps of the main house.

Something cold and wet tickled his face. In the few minutes they'd been inside, it had started to snow.

Lana and Logan danced around, hand in hand, laughing and looking upward. The sight clutched hard at Flint's chest.

"Come on down!" Lana called, laughter in her voice.

"Daddy! It's snowing!" Logan shouted, and ran back toward him.

Flint walked down the steps in time to catch Logan as he hurled himself into Flint's arms. The moment he was there he wiggled to get down, then grabbed Flint's hand and pulled him toward the road where Lana stood, smiling.

"Look, Daddy! Miss Alvarez says it's snow!"

Of course, they'd seen pictures of snow, had watched the weather channel when there was a blizzard in Colorado and had talked about their relatives plowing and shoveling their way out. But Logan had never seen it up close and personal.

They walked slowly down the lane together. Flint was very conscious of Lana by his side and felt the most absurd urge to put an arm around her. As if she were his woman. As if they were a family.

She's Logan's teacher! She's the temporary nanny! The voices in the back of his head were hopelessly drowned out by the sight of snowflakes gathering on Lana's dark hair and eyelashes.

She looked up at him and smiled. "Been a while since I've seen snow, myself."

"Me, too." He breathed in. Breathed out.

Logan ran back to them. "Can we build a snowman? Can we?"

Lana laughed and knelt down in front of Logan. "There's not enough snow for that, but here's what you can do. Try to catch snowflakes on your tongue." She demonstrated, sticking her tongue out and looking up at the sky.

"Cool!" Logan did the same, laughing as the snowflakes struck his face.

Flint was mesmerized. He couldn't have taken his eyes off Lana if his life depended on it.

She was, quite simply, gorgeous. Full of life. Stunning.

He was falling in love with her.

He blew out a breath and stared off into the distance, watching an edge of evening sun peek out between the clouds. When had *that* happened? Yeah, he liked and respected

Lana a lot. And, yeah, he'd been getting more attracted.

But love?

That was going to get him in a whole heap of trouble. That was going to break his heart, and maybe Logan's, too.

He looked upward, feeling the tiny cold tingles as the snow hit his face. *Need some help here, God.*

"Come on, we'd better head toward the house. We've got decorating to do," Lana said, rising to her feet. She and Logan headed toward the cabin, holding hands.

Flint blew out another breath and shook his head as he slowly fell into step behind them. This was bad. He had it bad.

He didn't want to fall in love. Didn't want to feel the heartache. Didn't want to take the risk.

"I don't want to go inside!" Logan yelled as they reached the cabin. He stopped beside the road and climbed the rail fence to perch on top. "Let's stay out here and watch it snow!"

Lana looked at Flint, signaling him with her eyes. Leaving it for him to decide.

That was a nice thing about Lana, he realized. She didn't mind speaking up when it was called for, but she also recognized that he, not she, was Logan's parent.

"We can stay out for a couple of minutes," he decided, "but then we need to do a little decorating and let Miss Alvarez go on home."

"Aw, Dad!"

He ruffled Logan's hair, halting the protest. "Shh. Let's enjoy this time while we have it. Make every minute count." He wasn't sure whether he was saying the words to Logan, to Lana, or to himself.

Chapter Ten

Wednesday afternoon, Lana swigged her diet soda and looked at Rhetta. "You ready?"

They were sitting at a small table off to the side of the teacher's lunchroom. Over at the big table, most of the other elementary school teachers were standing up, throwing away the remains of their lunches, gathering their things.

"No, I'm not ready." Rhetta pointed at her watch. "We still have four whole minutes!"

Lana laughed and leaned back. "Going to be a rough afternoon. Maybe we can take the first-graders into the gym for an hour, have them run off their energy."

"Called it already." Mrs. McKenna, a gray-haired second-grade teacher, turned around from the refrigerator and grinned. "When you've done the last day before Christmas break as many times as I have, you learn to think ahead. It's reserved for the next hour and a half for the second grade."

"Oh, great." Rhetta sighed. "My kids are going to be bouncing off the walls."

"Three more hours, and then, bring it on, Christmas break." Mrs. McKenna danced a little jig as she headed for the door.

The other teachers were clearing out, too.

"You got parents lined up to help at the party?" Rhetta asked.

"One of my four is sick, but two of the other ones are experienced. It'll be fine."

"I've got five scheduled. Can't have too much support. Who's new for you?"

Lana wrinkled her nose. "Logan's dad. Flint Rawlings."

Rhetta clapped a hand over her mouth. "He's doing the party?"

"Yeah. It's part of his attempt to give Logan more attention."

"How are things progressing between you two? Are you paying attention to your feelings, like I told you to?"

Lana rolled her eyes toward the ceiling. "Why does everyone try to match us up? I'm just Logan's temporary nanny!" But she knew why. Knew that she, at least, had a special energy whenever Flint was around.

Last night, after the snow had started falling, she and Logan and Flint had built a fire in the cabin and spent a couple of hours decorating. Which meant that she'd stayed for dinner—this time, with Flint cooking his famous Western omelets while she and Logan strung popcorn. Classical music had played in the background, and the evergreen branches they'd brought in had let out a piney scent, and it had been sweet and warm and wonderful.

"Spill it, girl," Rhetta ordered. "You're

looking way too dreamy for just a temporary nanny."

Lana shook her head. "I've been spending a lot of time with him, between taking care of Logan and working together on the Christmas pageant, but it's not ever going to come to anything."

"Oh? And why's that?"

"Because neither of us wants a relationship."

"You've talked about that?" Rhetta's voice rose to a squeak. "Don't you know that's the first step to having a relationship? Talking about your history and telling each other you can't possibly get involved?"

"It's not like that," Lana said, waving a hand. "He's really scarred by what Logan's mom did, abandoning him with a little baby. And you know me. The Lord meant me to be alone, and when I tried to go against that, I had the most humiliating experience of my life."

Rhetta shook her head. "That's going to be

a story you tell your grandkids. How you almost married the wrong man, but then you found Mr. Right. At which point, cue the romantic music, you look at your silver-haired but still gorgeous husband and smile and kiss under the mistletoe."

A vision of Flint as an older man flashed into Lana's mind. He'd go gray first at the temples, lending him a distinguished look. His time in the sun meant he already had tiny wrinkles at the corners of his eyes, but they just added to the character on his handsome face, kept him from looking like a pretty boy. That would just intensify as he got older...

She looked up to see Rhetta's amused grin. "Come on, daydreamer. I'm right and you know it. But we'd better get to those crazy kids. The bell's about to ring, and the lunch aides will have our hides if we're late."

Lana snapped her fingers. "Nature walk. Outside."

"Brilliant. I'm so there."

They headed toward the cafeteria, where

the din of excited kids was rising from high to deafening.

"Do you think Flint Rawlings knows what he's in for?" Rhetta asked, nodding toward the chaos ahead.

"He has no idea," Lana said as she walked into the fray.

Flint climbed out of his truck, slammed the door and then, when he saw another mother headed toward the school with a tray in her hands, opened the truck door back up. Couldn't forget the cupcakes. When one of the other party parents had emailed instructions, she'd assigned him to bake twenty-five cupcakes.

Which, first of all, didn't she know that cupcake pans came in twelves? That was what Marnie Binder had asked when she'd lent him a couple of tins.

She'd offered to bake them for him, too, but he'd actually taken the afternoon off so he could do things right, and he'd decided that baking his own would make a better statement to Logan.

Only, he'd gotten in a hurry because of having to wait while the one extra cupcake baked. And the frosting had looked fine when he'd opened the can, but once spread on the warm cupcakes, it had melted into nothing.

Oh, well, they would still taste good. And he'd looked up a craft online and stopped at the discount store to buy the supplies. He was all set.

Loaded down with Tupperware containers and shopping bags, he walked toward Logan's classroom, falling into step with another mother. The hallway reverberated with loud talking, shouts and laughter from the classrooms they passed. "Are they always this loud?" he asked the other mom.

"Wait until you get inside," she said, flashing a smile. "And first-graders are the worst. This is my sixth child, so I should know."

Inside Logan's classroom, Flint saw that

the chaos was, at least, organized. The children were all in their seats, although very wiggly, and Lana was leading them in a Christmas song.

"Keep going, children," she said when she saw the parents coming in, "but let's see who can sing the softest. Two whole verses that way!"

Gamely, the children tried to comply while Lana hurried to the door. "Whew, I'm glad you guys are here. Thank you so much for volunteering!"

"I'm used to it, that's why I'm taking the lead." A very blonde woman, dressed in Texas-tight jeans and high-heeled boots, whose name tag proclaimed her to be Jacqueline, stood up from the boxes she'd been kneeling over. "We're ready to...oh, wow. What happened to your cupcakes?"

"They'll taste good," Flint promised, setting them down on a table by the door.

"The kids will love anything sweet," Lana said distractedly. "Listen, if you're sure you've got it under control, I'm going to turn it over to you. Addy's aide wants to go help with her own son's party over in Room 8, so I need to help Addy navigate the party. She doesn't do that well with changes to her routine."

"No problem," said the mother Flint had walked in with, whose name was Aleesha. "Go ahead."

Lana headed over to a girl in a wheelchair, whose arms were waving. Her moans were audible over the sound of the children's increasingly loud singing.

Flint blinked and had to acknowledge that being a teacher was more of a challenge than he'd ever realized.

He tore his eyes away from Lana, who was comforting and distracting the child, to look at Jacqueline Blonde Boots and Aleesha. "I'm a novice at this," he said right away, wanting to keep their expectations in line. "I have a craft ready, but otherwise, I'll just do whatever you tell me to do."

"I suspect you're very competent," the

blonde woman murmured, leaning into his side in an unmistakable attempt at flirtation.

"Not competent at all." Blatant wasn't his thing, and he stepped away from her, which caused her to stumble a little.

She caught herself and gave him a dirty look. "Let's start with the snacks. That'll get their attention."

"It will get them full of sugar," Aleesha protested. "Should we maybe wait til the end for snacks?"

"I'm in charge of this party," Jacqueline said, eyeing Aleesha in unmistakable challenge.

Aleesha shrugged. "That's fine with me. You go for it."

"Thanks, I will. Because *she's* not going to be any help." Jacqueline was looking at Lana. "She's very young, isn't she?"

"I think she does a real good job," Flint defended Lana automatically.

Jacqueline sneered. "You *would* think so."

Whoa, he'd rather deal with cattle or de-linquent boys than room mothers any day.

"Kids," Aleesha said, clapping her hands. "Line up to wash hands. We're going to give you snacks first!"

The kids cheered and jostled and got into line, and Flint passed out napkins and his cupcakes while Jacqueline poured small cups of water and distributed chocolate candy. He'd heard her check with Lana about al-lergies, so he knew that wasn't a problem in this class, but he still had to question the wisdom of giving the kids so many sweets. Logan, for one, would be bouncing off the walls. But then again, Flint was just a party-novice dad. What did he know?

The kids finished the food in minutes and started getting out of their chairs and talk-ing loudly.

Flint rubbed the back of his neck, which was stiffening up. He had no idea how to proceed here, and Jacqueline had gone to the doorway to chat with another woman.

Logan started dragging Flint around, introducing him to his friends, explaining that his dad was a ranch foreman and could ride a horse. Flint fist-bumped and high-fived the kids as they walked around.

This made it all worthwhile. This was why he was here, for Logan, and he could put up with anything for...he sneaked a glance at the classroom clock...forty-five more minutes.

"All right, children," Jacqueline said, coming back into the noisy classroom. She flicked the lights, and the kids got quiet. "Time for your craft, and Mr. Rawlings is going to take charge of that!" She sat down at the edge of the classroom and crossed her arms.

Whoa. He was on.

"Okay, everybody sit in your seats." He knew that much. He went to the bag of stuff he'd brought and pulled out twenty packets of shoestrings. "Could you pass these out?" he asked Aleesha.

Then he broke open the first packet of

marshmallow Santas. "Now, everybody watch. What you're gonna do is make a necklace. Out of Santas. And Christmas trees, and reindeers." He held up a couple of other packets of marshmallow treats. "Like this." He poked the shoestring through the side of one Santa, pulled it on through, and added the next. Not much different from mending chaps. This was going great.

The kids started clamoring to do it themselves, so Flint just dumped the giant bag of marshmallow goodies on Lana's desk and told them they could each come up and get one.

He hadn't anticipated the stampede that followed. The packets were a little hard to get open, and one boy started crying because he'd had to take a packet of pink reindeers rather than the brown ones he'd wanted, but Aleesha smoothed that over and walked around with scissors, helping the kids open their packets.

Then one of the little girls started to cry.

She was close by Flint, so he squatted at her side. "What's wrong? Can't get the string through there?" he asked, holding out his hands to help with her necklace.

"I...don't wanna...stab Santa," she cried, putting her head down on her desk.

"I'll stab him for you! Take that, Santa!" The boy next to her jabbed his shoestring end into his marshmallow Santa with glee.

"I can stab better than that!" shouted another boy, pulling blunt-end scissors from his desk and pummeling his marshmallow reindeer with them.

The original crier started to wail, and the little girl behind her joined in. "I don't want to make a hole in Rudolph, either!"

A boy on the other side of that girl waved his hand vigorously. "Miss Alvarez, they're hurting Santa!"

Suddenly all the kids were yelling and crying and arguing. Were the marshmallow Santas real? Were the reindeer? Would Santa get mad at them for making the necklaces and stabbing him and his reindeer in the process? And if Santa's reindeer were hurt, would Santa still comc to their houses to leave presents?

Even standoffish Jacqueline was galvanized into action, wading in to try to calm things down. Dimly, Flint heard her reassuring children that they didn't *have* to stab Santa, that they could make a necklace out of marshmallow trees.

But although Jacqueline's voice, speaking to the children, was sugar-sweet, the side-eye she shot at him suggested she thought he was a Santa stabber himself. And her daughter, also pretty and blonde, wasn't any help. "*My* mommy wouldn't do a craft that was mean to Santa," she informed everyone within earshot, several times.

Aleesha, meanwhile, was busy with a group of boys, her own son included, who'd decided it would be fun to decapitate reindeer with the scissors from their desks. Aleesha had her lips pressed tight together and was shaking in an odd way, and finally Flint realized she was trying not to laugh.

Flint wasn't laughing, though, because Logan wasn't. He was tugging at Flint's arm. "Make them stop it, Dad!"

Flint felt about two inches tall.

He glanced over at Lana, but she was kneeling in front of the girl with the disability, who was sobbing. She already had her hands full.

This was a disaster. What had he been thinking, coming to volunteer in Logan's class?

Rhetta Douglass, a teacher he knew vaguely from town, stuck her head in the classroom door. "Everything okay in here?" she asked and then stepped inside. "Whoa. We were going to join our classes for the second half of the party, but on second thought, maybe I'll just take my kids back outside."

"We can take them outside?" Outside sounded like a huge relief to Flint, and the thought of it brought inspiration. He didn't know if it would work, but anything would be better than being stuck in this brightly colored prison with twenty-some crying, screaming first-graders.

"Okay, listen up!" he yelled in the voice he used to get the ranch boys' attention.

The room went immediately silent.

Flint blinked. "Line up and wash your hands, and then the moms are going to bring you outside. By the fence on the playground."

He looked at Aleesha to make sure at least one other adult was on board. She gave him a thumbs-up, so he left the classroom and the building double time. As he sprinted for his truck, he felt a deep longing to jump inside and head back to the ranch, where at least he knew what he was doing.

But that was the key: he had to stick to doing what he knew how to do. He didn't know if God answered the prayers of idiotic fathers completely out of their element, but he shot one up anyway: *Please, make this work. For Logan's sake.*

* * *

Lana pushed Addy's wheelchair toward the playground with trepidation. Most of the other children were running ahead, the classroom disaster forgotten. Aleesha, a lovely and easygoing room mother, slowed down to Lana's pace. "We'll get them doing something out here, and then I'll go clean up the classroom," she said, chuckling. "When I saw those children stabbing Santa... Oh, my. Only a father would think a craft like that could work."

"Let's hope he's got something better up his sleeve." Lana saw the children gathering around Flint at the playground fence. She felt guilty knowing she'd pushed Flint into volunteering to help with this party. And she should have recognized a recipe for disaster when she saw that Jacqueline Marsh was running the show.

"Wonder where he got all those ropes?" Aleesha asked.

Sure enough, Flint was tying loops into

ropes, talking the whole time, letting Logan wear his cowboy hat and stack the ropes neatly beside his dad. As she and Aleesha paused to watch, Flint did a breathtakingly graceful throw and roped the fence post.

"I want to try it!"

"Me, me!"

Flint held up a hand and shook his head, and the children fell silent.

"Good. Now, watch my wrist. It's all in the wrist." He demonstrated again. "Got that? Okay. Now it's your turn."

All of the children clamored to go first, but Flint, having apparently learned his lesson inside, organized them into groups and lined each one up by a fence post, safely far apart so that no one would get hurt. He put Logan, already a good roper, in charge of demonstrating to one group, and after a moment's conferring with Jacqueline, chose two more girls and a boy to lead the other groups—all ranch kids.

Addy moaned and wiggled, indicating that

she wanted to be a part of things, so Lana pushed her wheelchair closer while Alee-sha went back inside to put the classroom to rights. Lana didn't expect Flint to know anything about making an accommodation for Addy's disability, so she was surprised when he came over and squatted by Addy's wheelchair. "I saved a special rope just for you," he said, holding up a thin, lightweight rope with a loop at the end. "I need someone to rope that sage bush. Do you think you and Miss Alvarez could do that?"

Addy's arms moved up and down joyously, and Lana squatted to help the girl lasso the little bush, shooting Flint a smile. Of course. He worked with special kids all the time, at the ranch. It made sense that he would consider Addy's needs.

Flint moved over to offer advice and supervision to the rest of the children, and soon Lana saw him pulling aside a couple of smaller kids who were having trouble with the task. He spoke seriously with them, nodding over toward Lana and Addy.

The two children ran toward them. "Mr. Rawlings picked us out to come help Addy," they explained.

Perfect. Part of what Addy needed was companionship. Lana gave Flint a thumbs-up and got back a crooked smile in return.

It warmed her to the core, and made it difficult to focus on the three children in front of her.

Flint and Jacqueline supervised the kids lassoing, and the other children ran out their energy on the playground. By the time the buses started to arrive, the kids were able to settle and march back inside—to a neat classroom, thanks to Aleesha—to gather their things. Addy's aide returned to help the happy-looking girl prepare for her ride home.

As the children packed backpacks and jackets, chattering excitedly about Christmas and the vacation to come, Flint, Lana and Aleesha leaned against the chalkboard, watching. Jacqueline bustle among the children, helping and hugging them.

"I don't know how you do it," Aleesha said to Lana. "I'm worn-out from one hour with this many first-graders."

"Me, too." Flint wiped his face and hands with a bandanna. "I'm sorry I was such a dud as a room parent."

Lana patted his arm. "It was your first time. And besides, you ended up doing just fine."

"You rocked it!" Aleesha added. "My son, for one, will never forget this party."

"I kept thinking," he said, "that I could never do this on a daily basis. My heart would give out."

Lana laughed and then clapped her hands to get the kids' attention. "Boys and girls," she said, "what do we say to our party parents?"

"Thank you," they chorused. As they filed out, many stopped to hug Lana and the parents, including Flint. "That was awesome!"

and "Best party ever!" she heard from some of the kids.

"I'm teaching my little brother how to make these at home!" proclaimed little Brianna Dixon, holding up her half-completed, very sticky necklace.

"You do that," Flint said. Then as she left, Flint whispered to Lana, "Wasn't she one of the criers?"

"You never know with kids. They change moods faster than a desert chameleon changes colors."

"Dad, can I ride home on the bus?" Logan asked. "Mr. Smith said he'd give us candy if we behave."

"You bet," Flint said, ruffling Logan's hair. "You were a good helper today."

"So were you, Dad!" Logan said as he hurried after the line of children heading for the bus.

That made the women chuckle, but Flint blew out a breath, looking relieved.

"I'm going to take off, too," Aleesha said,

taking her son's hand. "I've gotta collect the rest of my kids. That was fun! Merry Christmas, everyone!"

"Tiffany, come on," Jacqueline said, gesturing to her daughter. "We have shopping to do!"

"Thanks so much for helping," Lana said to the departing families.

"No problem," Jacqueline said. "Bless your heart, you can call on me anytime you can't handle something yourself. At least *I* know how to run a party."

"Thanks." Lana held back a laugh as she watched the woman strut away.

She turned back into the empty classroom. Empty, except for Flint.

"Hey," he said immediately, "I'll get out of your hair, but I just wanted to apologize again. I underestimated what it would take to entertain a room full of kids. Lesson learned." He grabbed a couple of extra water bottles, held one out to her and took a long draw on the other one.

"The important thing is that Logan saw you were trying and you cared." Her worlds were melding. This was her classroom, where she was in charge; and yet here was Flint in the middle of it, doing his best, showing that he was a good dad. A good person. Her heart was getting way too warm toward him.

"I respect what you do. Even more now that I've tried it."

"Thanks."

They looked at each other for just a little too long. Flint was a quiet man, but he wasn't shy, and he didn't break eye contact. In fact, he stepped closer. "Lana, I…"

"What?"

He shook his head. "You sure are pretty," he said. "But even more than that, you have talent and heart. Don't let anyone put you down."

"I'll…try not to." She felt breathless.

And then there was more of that eye contact. When she licked her dry lips, his gaze flickered down and then back up. Lana's heart was pounding, her breath short. She was thinking of how close he'd come to kissing her.

But on the heels of that, she'd overheard him saying he wanted only to be single.

And then she'd spent the evening with him and Logan, and it had brought out all her longing.

Man, was she ever confused.

"Hey," Rhetta said, sticking her head in the door, "did everyone survive?"

"Barely." Flint grabbed his hat and headed for the door. "I was just telling Lana, I have the utmost respect for what you teachers do every day. Makes roping wild bulls look easy."

"Merry Christmas, cowboy," she said, watching him go.

And then she came over and perched on the desk beside Lana. "I'm sorry. Did I interrupt a moment?"

"No, of course not."

"Well? Did you flirt with him? Set up a date?"

"No date." Lana shook her head. "I'll admit, I wouldn't mind. But I have terrible judgment about men. I can't trust my feelings."

"You made one mistake," Rhetta said. "Are you going to let that rule your life? Love is wonderful and so, so worth it." She sighed. "When I think of what my life would be without Deron and the boys…"

"I'm not cut out for it," Lana broke in. "Sure, I wish I had what you have, but I'm not good at relationships."

"You're just being stubborn," Rhetta said. "I see how you look at him. And not only that, but I see how he looks at you. Are you going to stay single out of stubbornness, when God has dropped a wonderful man into your life?"

The words echoed in Lana's mind as she gathered her things and drove to the ranch. The boys had done so well at yesterday's rehearsal that she'd given them a night off from practicing today, allowing them to revel in their freedom from school for the next two weeks.

Flint had told her to take the night off, too, that he was off all day and was going to spend extra time with Logan.

She had a rare evening to herself. Rare, nowadays; she used to have evenings to herself as a matter of course and would have to hunt for things to do, take on extra projects.

Between the ranch and working for Flint Rawlings, her life had become pleasantly full. She wished it could continue that way.

But right now, she was exhausted, both from the crazy day at school and from the tension of being around Flint all the time, caring more than she should. She stopped for a fast-food salad on the way home, not wanting to do any cooking.

She'd soak in the tub and read the book she'd grabbed at the ranch library, one of the latest John Green novels for young adults.

She liked to keep up on books for teens, since the boys tended to come to her for recommendations.

As she turned into the ranch, she saw Flint and Logan putting up a Nativity scene in front of the main house. The figures were from a store, but the stable was one Flint had been making in the barn. She'd thought it was for the pageant, but now she realized that he'd made an extra one for the ranch.

Logan looked up admiringly at his father, and Flint was talking seriously to him. The sight of the two of them working together tugged at Lana's heart.

Flint and Logan's relationship was healing. They were closer than ever. She drove by slowly, not wanting to let them out of her sight.

If she'd helped a little bit with that healing, helped Flint see how to spend the time that Logan needed, then she'd done something good. Helped out in a way they needed.

They would go on fine without her. Oh,

Logan still clung on her some, and he'd still need female influences, a caregiver after school, for a good few years. But thinking of how Jacqueline Marsh had flirted with Flint, Lana knew that the handsome cowboy wouldn't have any trouble finding a mom for Logan if that was what he wanted. He was a good man. And now he was making an extra effort to be involved with his son. At the playground or the park, he'd be snatched up right away.

She needed to get comfortable with that fact and move on.

Chapter Eleven

The next day, Flint was mending a fence near the ranch house when Nick McGarrett strode toward him, toolbox in hand.

"Need some help?" Nick asked.

"Wouldn't turn it down." Nick was a good guy, a rancher trying to make it after his dad had run the family ranch way into debt while Nick was serving his country in Afghanistan. Not an easy life, but Nick didn't complain. In fact, he worked as the farrier for the boys ranch and helped out in other ways when he could. Flint was impressed that Nick made the time to volunteer, and after they'd gotten one length fixed and moved around the corner to the next broken section, he said so.

"Got a young friend I'd like to see come and live here. Promised his older brother I'd look out for him, and where he is, he's left alone too much of the time."

"What's his name?" Knowing one of the ranch kids had a brother who'd served would make Flint look out for him a little, too.

"Corey Phillips. Losing his big brother was hard on him. He's acting out."

Flint whistled. "His brother didn't come home? Where was he?"

"Afghanistan. A while back."

Nick didn't say more, but Flint could put it together. The boy's brother had been close to Nick, and he hadn't made it. "This place might be good for him. If he comes, I'll keep an eye on him."

They worked on in companionable silence for a while. It got warm enough that Flint took off his jacket and hung it on the fence.

A V of geese crossed the blue sky overhead, honking a greeting.

Over at the ranch house, a door slammed behind Fletcher Snowden Phillips, who stormed down the steps muttering to himself. Behind him, Bea Brewster opened the door back up and came out. She raised a hand like she was going to point a finger and lecture Fletcher, but ended up just planting her hands on her hips and shaking her head.

"Looks like he's in his usual tiff about nothing," Nick said as Fletcher marched to his late-model SUV—one of several vehicles he owned—got in and raised dust leaving the parking lot.

"Hope it's nothing. He's been threatening lawsuits against this place, and Bea looks upset. Truth is, if he wants to, he can stir up some real trouble."

"If he had a heart, he'd put some of that energy toward helping his less fortunate relatives." Nick pounded a nail extra hard. "But that's not gonna happen."

"What relatives?"

"Corey Phillips, for one. Who needs help Fletcher isn't willing to give."

"Seriously? The kid you were just talking about?"

"Yep." Nick turned away and focused on another part of the fence.

Up the path from the library Lana appeared, holding Logan by the hand, smiling as he talked a mile a minute. She held several books in one arm, and Logan was carrying a couple of picture books, too.

"Pretty sight," Nick said.

Flint glared at Nick, then deliberately went to fix a rail that put him between Lana and Nick.

Nick laughed. "Hey, brother, lighten up. I'm just admiring the scenery. I'm in no position to get interested in any woman."

"That's what I thought, too," Flint muttered, ripping savagely at a board. "That can change."

"I've neither time nor money for courtship," Nick said. "Too busy cleaning up my own family's messes to try to get involved with anybody else." His face twisted with a hint of bitterness.

Relieved, Flint nodded. "I hear that."

"Word around town," Nick said quietly, "is that you and Lana are…"

"Are what?" Flint eyed Nick. If people were talking, spreading rumors about Lana—

"That you're potentially a good couple." Nick dug in the toolbox and came up with some pliers. "Cool down, buddy! Nobody's trying to cut in on you. And nobody's talking trash about either of you. More like, wondering what's holding you back from taking it to the next level."

Flint blew out a sigh, rocked back on his heels and went back to prying at the rotting board. "Baggage. Bad history with women. Worried about Logan."

"Logan sure doesn't look worried." Nick nodded toward the ranch house, where Logan leaned comfortably against Lana's leg while she talked to Bea.

"Logan's six. He doesn't have a whole lot of sense."

"I knew your wife," Nick said unexpectedly. "We were classmates. Now her, yeah, I'd be worried about anyone getting involved with her. Lana's a whole 'nother story."

"She's good people." Flint was still suspicious of Nick's motives. He liked the guy, but he also knew how men were.

"You've got your life together. Good job, well respected, great kid. If you like her—" He nodded sideways toward Lana. "Why don't you go for it?"

Before Flint could come up with an argument, Marnie Binder spoke from just behind them. "He's right, you know. You'd better stop thinking Lana's going to leave town like your wife did and start courting her before one of the other cowboys around here takes your place." She held out a thermos. "Coffee. And here's some homemade fudge to keep you going."

"Thanks." Flint reached for the fudge at the same time Nick did. Flint snatched the tin container first and held it to his chest like a football. "Slowing down there?" he teased.

"I'm not the one who's slow."

Marnie held out a hand to high-five Nick. "If you don't do something to make this relationship move along, some of us will just have to help you do it." She sashayed back toward the ranch house.

"Marnie and her matchmaking." Flint opened the fudge container, holding it out to share the sweet treat.

After they'd downed some coffee and finished the section of fence they were working on, Nick headed off to do the evening chores at his own ranch.

But his words echoed in Flint's head. Why *didn't* he go for it? What was stopping him?

The argument about women not being trustworthy simply didn't hold water around Lana. She was one of the best people Flint had ever met, hands down. She thought of others, not herself, almost all the time, but she wasn't prissy or judgmental; instead, she was a lot of fun, lighthearted, genuine. There was a depth to her, too, that he didn't see in a lot of women her age. Maybe it was the problems she'd faced—losing her parents and then being left at the altar—that had given her a maturity and spirituality rare in anyone, let alone a twentysomething woman.

He was starting to trust her, he realized as he packed up his tools and headed for the barn. He trusted her not to hurt him and Logan on purpose. Not to leave them on a whim the way Logan's mother had. As he looked up at the blue sky overhead and thought about what Marnie and Nick had said, he made a sort of agreement. *All right, Lord. I'll consider it. I'm listening.*

"You and Flint are just...wow," Katie Ellis, the boys ranch receptionist, said to Lana later that evening.

"Wow?" Lana asked absently. She was hanging up costumes that had just been delivered, hoping to get the wrinkles out without ironing. Everything had to be in place for the dress rehearsal later tonight.

"You have something so special." Katie sighed. "I can just see it in his eyes when he looks at you, how he cares for you."

"You have a good imagination," Lana said briskly. She was so used to having this argument with herself that opening it up to another person didn't even faze her. "Flint and I are becoming friends, but that's all it'll ever be."

"I heard that, and it's ridiculous!" Rhetta Douglass walked into the barn, with Macy Swanson right behind her. "We're here to help you get ready for the dress rehearsal. What do you need us to do?"

"Besides talk you into going out with Flint," Macy added.

Lana threw up her hands. "He hasn't asked me out, okay? He's my boss. He's the parent of a kid in my class. He's my temporary neighbor."

"Still…" Katie trailed off.

Rhetta was nodding vigorously. "That doesn't mean you can't—"

"Stop!" Lana put her hands on her hips and glared at both women. "What word did you *not* hear in my description of our friendship? Date, right? We're not dating!"

Rhetta raised her eyebrows at Macy and Katie. "Well, well. *Somebody* feels strongly about this issue."

"I don't feel strongly!" Lana exclaimed. Then, she heard herself and let out a big sigh.

There was no getting away from it, and no hiding it from her friends, either. She felt more for Flint than anyone should feel for a boss or a student's father. She looked at him, especially lately, in a decidedly unprofessional way.

The other three women circled her, arms crossed.

"Come on," Rhetta said. "Tell us what's going on. And don't you dare say 'nothing.'"

"I need my privacy," Lana protested, but she felt the beginnings of a smile.

"You need your girlfriends," Macy said. "Believe me, falling in love is *not* something you should be going through alone."

"I'm not falling in love! But okay. I like Flint a lot, and I'm crazy about his son."

"And you'd like things to go further. Right?"

"How am I supposed to answer that?" Lana sat down on a hay bale, chin propped on her fist.

"Tell the truth," Macy suggested.

"Believe in romance." Katie sighed. "Like I would, if Pastor Andrew only gave me the time of day."

"We'll deal with your issue another time," Rhetta promised. "Right now, we're going to focus on Lana. Make her see reason."

"I do see reason," Lana protested. "I know what I know. Flint doesn't ever want to marry again. For me to get all focused on him would be a huge mistake."

"How do you know that?" Katie asked. "Because the way he looks at you…"

"You're a romantic. You see hearts and flowers everywhere."

"I see it, too," Macy said frankly. "I think he'd go for you if you'd give him half a chance."

Lana couldn't help feeling a little surge of hope. If other people were seeing Flint's feelings for her, then they must exist. Right?

But even if he had feelings, he also had plans, and Flint was nothing if not strong-willed.

"He's decided not to marry again." Lana recounted what she'd heard Flint say in the feed store. "He wasn't saying it for effect. He was speaking the truth. To a close friend."

Rhetta waved her hand. "Men never want to be pinned down," she said, looking at Macy. "Right?"

"Right. Until they do want to." Macy giggled. "Tanner was bound and determined he wouldn't marry someone like me. And look at us now!" She held up her left hand, sparkling with a beautiful diamond.

"I don't buy it." Lana held out a cooler of sodas to the other women. "And I can't risk it. I pressured someone into marrying me before, and look what happened. He backed out at the last minute. I'm not going through that again."

"Flint would never back out," Macy said. "He's loyal to the core. And you care about each other. It's obvious! We just need to find a way to help you along."

"How about the mystery matchmakers?" Katie suggested with a smile. "They've been setting up families like crazy, and you, Flint and Logan are a perfect match."

Lana shook her head. "Believe me, they've been on the case. But even they don't want me to get together with Flint. They're trying to match me up with other guys in town. They probably know the truth—Flint's just not the marrying kind."

"Show a little faith, honey." Macy beckoned to the others. "Come on, we have a couple of things to do in the ranch house." They left the barn, talking and giggling.

After they left, Lana sat down at a little table to fold the programs Bea had gotten printed in the office.

Could she have a relationship? Was Flint's reluctance really just a guy thing? If he, deep inside, wanted to go ahead with something between them, could she join in?

Outside the barn, she heard the murmur of voices; it sounded like Marnie had stopped to talk with someone, and there was Rhetta's deep chuckle. She heard a boy yelling, then another, the sound of running feet. That would be Logan, burning off some steam before dinner.

If she were to start up a relationship, she would want to do it with Flint. She could acknowledge that now. Somewhere in the past few days and weeks, seeing how hard he worked and tried, admiring his leadership on the ranch, noticing his care for Logan... Yeah. It had gotten to her.

She'd at least halfway fallen in love. Maybe more than halfway.

She hugged herself and leaned against the half wall of one of the stalls. Love. Against her will and her best intentions, she'd fallen in love.

"You okay?" Flint Rawlings's voice startled her, and he materialized in the barn's dimness. He was carrying a rope and the heavy Christmas star some of the older boys had made for the pageant, at school in their woodworking class.

She felt herself blushing and was glad for

the low light. Could he read her thoughts, see the foolish expression on her face?

"Lana?" He walked closer. "Is something wrong?"

"I'm fine," she said quickly. "Just working on the programs. We're about all set up for the dress rehearsal." Whew. She sucked in her breath, smelling hay and wood and the pungent scent of turpentine.

He nodded and put down what he was carrying. Then, hands on hips, he turned back to her. "So what's left to do? I'm here to help, if you need me."

He sounded relaxed, more relaxed than he had in a while. He wasn't nervous. He hadn't just had a revelation, as she had.

"I just need to get us set up for the first scene. And hang the star."

He nodded and rolled up his sleeves. Having been here throughout the rehearsals, he seemed to know what to do. They worked together, moving the props into place for the roadside scene, where Joseph and Mary would walk toward Bethlehem, passing shepherds and sheep on the way.

Flint was a man used to hard work, and he did it without complaint, even with a smile. After a full day of working the ranch, he still took time to help with the pageant, quietly doing what was needed, without complaint and without any expectation of gratitude.

But she *was* grateful. "That about does it," she said after they'd gotten the scene into place. "Thank you so much for your help."

"Sure that's all you need?"

"Well…there's just the star to hang. I don't think I can do that alone."

"You shouldn't. That's what we males are for."

"That's sexist," she said automatically.

"Just accept it. We guys like to help a pretty lady."

Was he flirting with her?

She felt her face heating. Time to get businesslike. "Okay, so I want it as high as possible up over the stable. It's nice and big, so everyone can see it, especially if we shine a spotlight on it."

"At your service." He disappeared into the barn's storage room and emerged with a tall stepladder. He set it up behind the stable and climbed up, balancing on the top rung and holding the star for her to see. "Around about here, or higher?"

For an absurd moment, Lana imagined that they were married and hanging pictures in a new house. She'd be trying to get everything to look perfect, a wonderful home for them and Logan. Flint would be patient, as he was now; waiting, good-natured about it; he'd be a good partner in decorating as in so many other things.

She fanned herself with the small stack of pageant programs she'd picked up. "Maybe up a little higher?"

He was about to step up higher when she saw the ladder wobble. "Just a minute, wait." She grabbed a chair and pulled it over, climbed up on it.

She meant to just steady the ladder, but somehow her hands ended up holding his muscular, jean-clad legs. He went still for a moment, then hitched the star up higher, tossed a rope over a rafter, and hung the star. "Just one more sec and this'll be secure. Then you can look at it and see if it suits your fancy." His voice sounded a little tight.

When she was sure he wasn't going to fall, she let go of his legs and held the ladder, and a moment later, he was climbing down.

He reached the floor and immediately held out a hand to help her down.

Lana's heart beat faster than it should as she stepped from the chair, holding his hand for balance. "I'm supposed to be helping *you*."

His eyes held hers for a little too long, and he didn't drop her hand. "We can help each other."

Golden light slanted through the boards on the western side of the barn, revealing the dust motes that danced in the sun's rays. Flint's words seemed to be fraught with meaning.

Lana blew out a breath. It was getting *very* warm in here. She tugged her hand away from his and backed up to inspect the star.

Flint went over to the small, rudimentary light board and fiddled with the switches. A spotlight came on, illuminating the star, which she could now see had been beveled and painted with sparkly paint. The star glowed, turning a little in the warm air.

She couldn't restrain a little hand clap. "It's beautiful!"

Flint came to stand behind her, close but not touching her. "Doesn't look half bad."

As she watched it, the star seemed to twinkle.

"You okay with the placement? Want me to move it?"

"It's good," she said, half turning around. "It's perfect. I was just thinking about…the star of Bethlehem and what it represents. New life."

"New hope," he said, nodding. "I've been thinking about that some, too."

She hazarded a glance at him. "Have you?"

He reached out a hand and, with a gentle touch on her shoulder, turned her around to face him. He left his hand there, warming her shoulder.

They were standing very close together, close enough that she caught the woodsy, leather smell that always seemed to be a part of Flint.

"I feel a lot for you, Lana," he said. "That's another thing I've been thinking about."

"What do you feel?" She was breathless.

He studied her, their eyes tight on each other. She couldn't look away.

He did, though, and stepped back. "Thinking I'm not exactly right for someone like you," he said. "Thinking I'm kind of old and beat-up for someone as young and pretty as you are."

She laughed. "Yeah, you seem so old

when you scramble around the rafters like a monkey."

One side of his mouth quirked up. "I don't feel old. In fact, sometimes I feel more like a teenage boy who's just fallen for a girl and doesn't know how to handle it."

Fallen for a girl. Had he *fallen* for her? What else could he mean?

Her heart gave a great, joyous thump, and she reached out both of her hands, grasped his bigger, callused ones. "I've fallen for you a little bit, too."

"Oh, really?" He looked into her eyes as if reading her sincerity. Then he looked at her lips.

And then he pulled her close and brushed his mouth over hers.

It was the sweetest kiss Lana had ever felt. Partly because she could tell he was holding back. His shoulder muscles, under her hands, were tight, and he used his hands to keep her at a safe distance.

But even with all of his safeguards, the kiss burned her like fire.

She pulled one of her hands free to touch her own lips, her eyes wide as she looked at him. "Did that mean…"

"It means I want to—"

All of a sudden, the barn door behind them slammed shut.

They jumped apart in the sudden darkness. "Now, what's that all about?" Flint asked.

"Kids playing, I'd bet." It had happened before, a couple of times in rehearsal. "Or…" She snapped her fingers. "Rhetta and the girls, matchmaking."

"Or Marnie Binder." There was a smile in his voice.

She started toward the door, feeling her way, but Flint touched her arm. "Wait a second."

"Yeah?" She looked up at him and saw his eyes had darkened.

"I was always taught to seize opportunities," he said. "When you're the younger of a bunch of brothers, you do that. How about if I kiss you again?"

He was letting her decide, and she almost wished he hadn't, because she didn't want to think about what it all might mean and all the reasons they shouldn't do it. But he'd placed the responsibility on her, and she was nothing if not responsible. "I don't know if I can..."

"We're both a little scarred, Lana. We can't move fast, and I don't expect to. But I'm thinking, maybe, we should move toward something together."

Her heart pounded hard, and her stomach swarmed with butterflies, and she couldn't speak. But she gave a little nod, and immediately his hands came up to cradle her face. His thumb touched her lip, light as a bird's wing. "So pretty," he said. "Wow, you are *so* pretty."

And then he lowered his head to hers and pulled her close. And this time, the kiss wasn't gentle and sweet. Flint still held himself back, but the passion and the promise left her trembling.

New life, she thought wildly as he broke the kiss and pulled her against his shoulder, both of them breathing hard. Was she ready for it?

Chapter Twelve

Flint was wired as tight as a new army recruit as he slid open the barn door, one arm still around Lana's shoulders.

That had been some kiss.

He was tense from holding himself back, but lit up from the bright possibilities opening up in front of him. As bright as the glow of the setting sun, which momentarily blinded him as he slid a hand down to the small of Lana's back and walked outside.

The voices brought him back, though. There were the women, standing over by the fence, Marnie and Rhetta on one side, Macy and Katie on the other, leaning together in that way women had when they were sharing secrets.

Pastor Andrew—for whom Flint could feel nothing but good-heartedness, now that he knew Lana wasn't interested in him—stood talking to Tanner.

A murmur went around the group, and everyone turned to look at them. And for once, Flint didn't care that everyone could guess their business, that the fact that they'd been kissing was probably written all over their faces.

Logan turned away from the other boys and the racetrack they'd built in the sand. He jumped up and ran toward them, leaping, barely able to contain himself. His words spilled out, loud and clear: "Is it true, is it true, are you getting married? Is Miss Alvarez going to be my mom?"

"What?" Flint squatted down to catch him. "No. No, son." Logan had this tendency to get ahead of himself. What Flint and Lana were discovering about each other was so new. Flint didn't want to threaten it by moving too fast. "You know what family is, and she's not a part of it. It's just you and me." He chuckled as he hugged his crazy, over-imaginative son.

Behind him, Lana gasped. She must be as surprised by the question as he was.

The others, kids and adults, had all turned toward them, but Flint was focusing on Logan's face, which had fallen. Flint opened his mouth, trying to think of how to explain to a six-year-old the delicate pacing of adult relationships.

He glanced back at Lana, wanting to give her a look that said they'd talk later. His own face was still curved in a smile, remembering what had just happened.

But Lana's face had gone pale. "Not…a part…" She trailed off.

What did she mean? What was wrong?

She looked around, and he did, too. Saw that everyone in the barnyard had stopped their own conversations and were watching them. He wished they weren't.

"What's wrong?" he asked.

She lifted a hand like a stop sign, physically cutting him off. The expression on her face grew hard. It was a look he'd never seen her wear.

"No, I'm not part of the family," she said, not to Logan but to the small crowd around them. "I might not even be here that long. I have a job offer for next year, in Dallas."

A tiny sound from Logan drew Flint's attention. Even as he was taking in the upset expression on his son's face, Flint mentally replayed Lana's words. "I might not even be here that long…job offer for next year… Dallas."

Did worst nightmares really rear their heads and turn into reality in daylight? Because this was his. He'd let Lana in, and it was exactly like when his wife left, even down to her destination.

He pulled Logan to his chest. The voices that rose around them faded to a dull roar.

She was leaving. Leaving him and Logan, just as Logan's mother had.

He felt Logan's chest shake in a little sob and patted his back, his own heart breaking. What had that been about in the barn? Had she known she was leaving, even while she was kissing him?

There was a hand on his shoulder, another on Logan's. "Come on, Logan," Marnie Binder said. "You promised you'd help me pass out the cookies."

"We need to shove off," Tanner said to Macy. There were more murmurs, more departures.

"You two need to talk," he heard Rhetta say to Lana. Then she gestured to Katie, and they both headed back toward the ranch house.

"I'm not talking to him," Lana muttered, too low for Rhetta to hear, but loud enough for Flint. "I've walked this road before."

So had he.

"Come on with me," Marnie said to Logan, gently disengaging him from Flint's arms.

Which left Flint and Lana alone.

He looked up in time to see her spin away from him and march back into the barn.

He stood up and headed away, toward trucks and horses and equipment. Things he understood.

The smell of sage and the fertile earth pushed into him, and he managed to take a deep breath, then another. Looking up, he saw a small shed that had needed taking down for a while. Logan and the other young boys sometimes played there, but it wasn't safe.

He strode into the barn, found an ax and went back out to the shed. There was a right way to take down a building, but he didn't have time for that. This was small. He'd just chop it down himself, get it done.

Cowboy appeared at his side, offering a

little whine, but Flint nudged the dog away with his leg. He didn't really want comfort.

He pounded hard, watched one side crash in. The smell of rotting wood rose up.

Lana's face seemed to swim before his eyes. Soft with emotion, a gentle, awakening passion, as he'd kissed her. Hard with bitterness, saying she was leaving town.

It didn't compute.

But over all of that, he couldn't erase the sight of Logan's stricken expression.

He swung the ax harder, bringing down the next wall of the shed. He'd been an idiot. He'd truly fallen for her. And he'd put his son at emotional risk by doing it.

From the direction of the storage barn, he heard shouts and laughter. The dress rehearsal must be starting. Cowboy's ears pricked up, and he trotted off toward the action.

A tiny surge of guilt flashed through him. They might need him. Logan might need him.

But, no, Logan was with Marnie, and soon

he'd play his role in the pageant. He'd stay near Lana, anyway. He adored her.

Lana must be fine, carrying on the rehearsal. Of course she was. She was a responsible person, a caring one.

Even in the pain of how she'd rejected him—and rejected Logan, he thought, swinging the ax viciously—he couldn't paint her as a bad person. He knew she cared for others, did for them, took care of them.

She just didn't care for *him*.

He leaned his forehead against the one piece of the shed wall remaining upright and shut his eyes. His chest burned. This was what heartache felt like.

And the hurt was so much deeper than when Stacie had left them. Because then, Logan had been mercifully unaware of the abandonment, being only a few weeks old.

But there was another reason Lana's departure hurt so much worse.

It was because Flint loved her so much more.

He'd been young when he'd married Stacie, infatuated with her good looks and exciting personality, proud to have her on his arm. He'd loved her, sure, but in an immature way that had more to do with externals than with the things that mattered.

Lana was also beautiful, even more beautiful than Stacie had been. But her appeal went deeper, to her sweet spirituality and caring heart. Lana was the kind of woman you could grow old with, a woman whose appeal wouldn't fade when her hair was gray and her waistline thickened. Because it wasn't about looks. It was the whole person.

He stared down at the dirt and saw something sparkle. He reached down and picked it up.

A gold hoop earring. One Lana had lost a few days ago.

It made him remember seeing her and Logan here outside the shed, sitting on the ground with a little napkin spread in front of them, having a pretend picnic. Logan had told him later that they'd been playing house, and Flint had stifled his own reaction of "that's no game for a boy." If Lana thought it was a valid game for Logan, that was good enough for him. He trusted her judgment.

He closed his fist around the earring, feeling its point dig into his palm. How much she'd given him and Logan in this short time. She'd helped a sad little boy feel like he had a family. She'd taught Flint more about being a dad than he had learned in the previous five years of single parenting.

Man, he'd miss her.

They'd both miss her.

A groan came from deep in his chest and found release, and then he grabbed up the ax again. He couldn't stand out here yelling, scaring the boys. Had to put his energy to good use.

He swung the ax and the last pillar of the shed crashed to the ground.

He'd had the plan to be independent, to raise Logan alone, this whole time. He'd insisted on it, taken pride in it. Even when

Lana had come, he'd told himself he'd rather be alone, that he and Logan had no need of a woman's touch in their lives.

Now, that plan of solitary independence felt like a prison sentence. When had his view of marriage—of a lifelong try at love with a woman—morphed from "never again" to "maybe…as long as it's Lana?"

Only now, Lana didn't want him.

He looked at the demolished shed. What a mess. He'd have to clean it up before the boys got into the splintery boards and rusty nails.

He sighed, bent down, and picked up a load to carry toward the dumpster. He tossed it in, still feeling like there was a hole in his heart.

Over at the storage barn, lights flashed and music played.

He should go over there. But he was pretty much unfit for human consumption.

He blew out a breath and looked up at the sky, now filled with a glittering array of stars.

Walked back on over to the remains of the

shed and sank down onto his knees, thinking to grab another load.

Looked up at the sky again and felt like a small man, made of nothing but despair.

Maybe on his knees was the right place to be.

Friday night, Lana went through the motions of preparing to direct the Christmas pageant. She calmed down nervous performers, stitched together rips in costumes, and welcomed the early arrivals, some from the community and some parents from farther away.

All the while marveling that no one could tell she was nursing a broken heart.

She kept replaying last night in her mind. She hadn't slept for replaying it, trying to understand, to figure out how things had gone so wrong so quickly.

One minute, she and Flint had been kissing in the barn, talking of a promising future.

The next minute, he'd excluded her from his family in front of a crowd of people.

Did she have a "jilt me" sign printed on her back, or what?

She just couldn't believe it. She'd seen the caring, even love in his eyes, not just when he'd kissed her, but earlier and often. She'd tried not to recognize it, but some part of her had known it was there, known it enough to let her own heart follow suit.

It just didn't make sense.

Flint wasn't the kind of man who'd lie to a woman just to get a little affection. He was good and upright and moral; she knew that.

And yet, he'd stated in front of all those people that she wasn't a part of his family, that it was just him and Logan. There hadn't even been a question in his voice.

His declaration had pretty near broken Logan's heart, too; she'd seen the pain in the boy's eyes as he'd realized his dream of a mom was going down the tubes. Flint wouldn't have hurt Logan unless he'd really meant what he'd said.

Ever since, Logan had avoided her. She'd seen him running around with some of the ranch boys, but he wasn't his usual self.

She'd texted Flint to see if he needed her to care for Logan today and had received an abrupt "no, thanks" in response.

Which had left her to spend the day in her little apartment, crying her eyes out.

Toward midafternoon she'd forced herself to wrap presents. She had pretty scented candles for Marnie, Katie and Macy. For Rhetta, who didn't get much time to indulge herself, she'd made up a basket of bath oils and lotions and had tucked in a handmade certificate offering a couple of hours of babysitting.

She'd splurged on a nice Lego construction set for Logan, knowing it was the type of thing he could enjoy alone or with his father.

For Flint, she'd ordered his favorite author's latest hardback, because she'd noticed he mostly read paperbacks from the used bookstore. Like any single parent, he was on a budget.

But when she'd pulled it out to wrap, it had seemed valueless, boring. The kind of gift an about-to-be-dumped girl would get for a guy she was crushing on. And what could she write on the card, anyway?

A few more people came in through the barn's sliding doors, a welcome distraction from her melancholy thoughts.

The barn came back into focus, and she smelled the familiar aroma of sweaty boys, along with the fragrant pine boughs someone had brought in.

She crossed the barn to where Bea was chatting with some of the other parents and touched her shoulder. She nodded sideways toward the new arrivals. "Are they okay?" she asked quietly.

It was a sad reality of working with the at-risk boys on the ranch; some of their parents and guardians were barred from contact with their children. The boys ranch was a small enough operation not to post a guard at the door, but Bea, who knew every detail of every boy's situation, kept a sharp eye on who came and went and urged everyone else to do the same.

Bea looked over toward the entrance, frowned and stood, making a quick excuse to the parents she'd been chatting with. She stepped to Lana's side. "That's Sam Clark's dad, and he shouldn't be here. I don't recognize the other guy. Text Flint, will you? Just in case I need some backup."

Lana did it, wondering if he'd even answer. He'd made himself scarce in the past twenty-four hours. And a text from someone you'd just dumped wouldn't likely be high on the "eager-to-open" list.

As she hit Send, the question about the identity of the second man was answered.

"Papa!" Robby Gonzalez cried, and ran across the barn to throw his arms around the stoop-shouldered man.

Mr. Gonzalez hugged Robby hard. Then

he pulled back and put his hands on his son's shoulders. Lana couldn't hear what they were saying, but the obvious emotion of the scene made tears rise to her own eyes.

Bea was speaking to the other man, and that conversation didn't appear to be going so smoothly. Automatically, Lana looked around for Sam and saw him quietly watching. Unlike Robby, he hadn't run to throw himself into his father's arms. That could be a difference in their personalities—Robby was very outgoing, while Sam was shy, almost backward—or it could mean difficulties in the family relationship. Unfortunately, that was the case with a good number of the boys here.

She saw the boy swallowing hard and went to him. "Hey," she said, sitting down on the edge of the stage to be closer to his size. "Guess your dad wanted to see you perform, huh?"

Sam shrugged and looked away.

"He might not be allowed to stay, if the

judges and courts have made that rule for now," she said. "But you could write him a letter if you wanted. We could send him a picture of you in the pageant."

Sam nodded quickly, glancing at her and then at the heated conversation between Bea and his father.

"For now," she said, "run and ask Mrs. Binder to help you with your shepherd's costume. It's almost time to start." She patted his arm.

He looked almost relieved to have something to do. He even gave her a brief, shy smile as he hurried backstage.

Lana looked back toward the door in time to see Bea escorting Mr. Clark out.

Meanwhile, there was Flint, speaking quietly to Robby and his father.

He looked up and their eyes met. He gestured her over.

Absurd hope rose in her, and she shoved herself off the stage and started toward them. Cool it. Don't run like an idiot. It's probably nothing.

When she reached the trio, she noticed a muscle working in Flint's cheek.

"Could you translate for Mr. Gonzalez and me?" he asked. "I'm trying to explain the rules, and it's a little complicated." He gave a subtle nod toward Robby, whose eyes were shiny with tears.

Clearly, Robby was having trouble telling his dad he couldn't stay for the show. That was understandable, and Lana's momentary hurt that Flint just wanted her for her Spanish-speaking abilities dissolved in the emotions this struggling family was obviously feeling.

She greeted Mr. Gonzalez in Spanish and was rewarded by an emotional explanation of how he'd just returned from a long stint in Mexico, where he'd been working for an agricultural operation deep in the back country. Communication hadn't been good, and he had only now realized what trouble Robby, his wife and his other children were having. "I came as quickly as I could," he explained. "We would like to take Robby home, but he thinks there are rules that won't allow it."

"That's right." Lana explained gently that, right now, Mr. Gonzalez wasn't on the approved list and couldn't stay for the pageant. "We're taking a lot of pictures," she promised, "and we'll send them to you. And Miss Bea will work with you on resolving the family issues. We aren't trying to keep your son for a bad reason. The ranch helps boys, and he'll come home stronger."

After a little more conversation and some translation for Bea when she came back, they all hugged. Mr. Gonzalez left, and Robby ran to get on his costume, unashamedly crying but with a big smile on his face.

Lana couldn't restrain her own smile. Scenes like that made everything they were doing worthwhile. She was sure that family would be back together soon, with Robby's challenging times behind him.

She looked over, instinctively wanting to share this moment with Flint, but he was gone.

Her heart seemed to dry up and wither inside her, causing her chest to heave a little with the hurt.

She couldn't take this. She would have to move to Dallas for real. She couldn't be close to him, feeling all this longing and wishing that could never come true.

Around her, recorded Christmas music started into her favorite Christmas song, "Good King Wenceslas." She remembered a Sunday school teacher reading the class a storybook about the famous king and his quest to relieve the sufferings of the poor.

Some day, very soon, she'd be able to content herself with a life spent giving to others. She wouldn't worry about getting love in return. It was the kind of life she'd settled on once her wedding had gone south, but Flint Rawlings and his son had poked a hole in that contentment.

She'd get it back. But not tonight. She straightened her shoulders and walked toward the stage.

Macy came down to her. "You okay?" she asked. "You're not looking so good. It's about time to start, but if you need me to do the opening..."

"No, I can do it." She drew in a breath and forced a little smile at Macy. "Are the boys ready?"

"They will be after your introduction." A smoky smell came from backstage, and Macy rolled her eyes. "I *told* Colby not to light that incense yet. I'd better go back there to supervise."

Lana nodded and drew in another deep breath. Sent up a prayer for composure. And then she climbed the steps to the stage and walked over to the podium, looked out at the expectant audience, clad mostly in red and green, and welcomed them to the pageant.

Of course, the unfolding story and the cute, sometimes moving efforts of the young actors swept her away from her own concerns. The audience clapped and cheered for each of the three short acts, and some wiped tears when the ragtag boys offered their final message.

As the applause arose, Lana blew out a sigh. God was good.

He has more for me than I ever expected.

She remembered when that thought had come to her, wiping away her fears that her life wasn't going to amount to anything, wasn't going to give her much, if any happiness.

It had all been connected with Flint.

But had she been wrong about that? The Creator was, indeed, bigger than their small human minds could know.

Had she misinterpreted what Flint had said? Had she been too sensitive in feeling that he was dumping her?

She started to replay the scene in her mind but shook off the impulse. Now wasn't the time. The boys were approaching the stack of presents from the community, a stack almost as tall as the smallest boys' heads.

She loved it here. Loved that the community cared so much for these troubled boys. She looked around and marveled at how many adults in town had volunteered their time to make this event a success, to help boys like Sam Clark, who wouldn't get to go home, have a fun Christmas.

As Bea and Marnie distributed the gifts, she watched the boys joyously rip into them and exclaim over them. Most of the boys looked thrilled even when the package they opened held a pair of socks or a new bandanna.

Nostalgia for when she was a little girl rose in her. She remembered that joy. Her family hadn't been wealthy, and there hadn't been fancy gifts around the tree, but the festive wrapping and the happy faces of loved ones had made Christmas the best day of the year.

She had those memories stored up inside her, rendering Christmas blessed and happy even though her parents weren't here to share the day. Hopefully, these boys would recall this night as a happy memory. They'd focused on the true meaning of Christmas… and they were also getting some fun and desired presents.

Someone tapped her shoulder, and she turned to see a huge poinsettia plant in a beautiful basket. She reached for it automatically and saw that it was Bea holding it out to her. "This is from all of us," she said. "Just a token of how thankful we are for all your hard work."

"There's another bouquet over here," one of the boys called, and then a much smaller bouquet was thrust in her hands. On this one, there was a tag made of notebook paper attached.

"From Flint," it read.

Her heart jumped for a few seconds, and then she realized what was going on and forced a chuckle. "Those mystery matchmakers," she said to Bea. "Looks like they've changed their minds about who I should be with."

"They're smart boys," Bea said, giving her a meaningful look.

Lana couldn't stop the tears that rose into her eyes, so she busied herself with carrying her giant poinsettia to the door, setting it down beside her bag and tucking the other flowers into the pot.

People were drifting out now, congratulating her on a job well done. A number of the boys were heading to the ranch house to get their things, because they were leaving with their families tonight for the Christmas holiday. Others would be picked up tomorrow, and a few boys would stay over the break, because their situations didn't permit them to go home for Christmas.

"Lana." She heard Flint's deep voice behind her and turned, her heart flipping over when she saw him walking toward her with intent. This was crazy. She was on such an emotional roller coaster. It was probably nothing, some detail. "Hey," she said as he reached her side, taking a deep breath and inadvertently inhaling the scent of him. She swallowed hard.

And then she saw the wrinkles of concern on his brow. "Have you seen Logan?" he asked.

"Not since his appearance in the pageant."

Flint let out a muffled expression of concern. "Neither has anyone else," he said. "I'm afraid he's missing."

Chapter Thirteen

It took about five minutes for every person on the ranch who hadn't already left for the holidays to gather at the barn and organize a search. Most of them were chuckling and rolling their eyes; they all knew Logan's history of running and hiding, making this more comical than something to worry about. Still, it was nighttime, so they fanned out, some to the ranch house, some to the various barns and play areas, some to Flint's cabin.

Flint paced the barn, searching dark corners, overwhelmed with guilt. He hadn't been watching Logan, but rather wallowing in his own distress about Lana's leaving. He'd let down his son on so many levels.

Lana, who'd looked tired and drawn all night, was using her phone to field everyone's reports. "He's not at the library. Not at the house with the other boys. We're still waiting to hear from those who are searching the barns and your cabin."

"Thanks." He grabbed a flashlight, went to the stage, and shone it underneath.

"He runs away pretty often, right?"

"Yes, but I thought he was over it. We're back to square one."

"Kids regress," she said. "The holidays are stressful for them."

He nodded, wondering fleetingly why Lana had been so upset-looking all day. Wasn't she happy about her plan to leave?

Marnie Binder came in just as Lana reported the next news: no sign of Logan in the barns or the cabin.

His worry intensifying, Flint grabbed a

rake and went over to the end stalls that still had hay in them, raked through.

"Flint." Lana came into the stall, grabbed the sleeve of his shirt, and tugged him out into the open part of the barn where Marnie was. "Stop moving for a second and think. You're the one who knows him best. Figure out where he might be!"

Flint blew out a breath as the truth came to him: his plan to raise Logan independently, not to need anyone else, was a pipe dream. It took a village. Plus God.

Bea and Rhetta came hurrying back into the barn. "We didn't find him," Bea said quickly. "But we're wondering—have you seen Cowboy?"

He hadn't. Flint put his fingers to his mouth and did Cowboy's special whistle, piercing enough for the dog to hear anywhere on this section of the ranch.

They all waited, but there was no answering bark, no excited dog hurtling into the barn.

"Do you think he might have hidden out

with Cowboy somewhere?" Bea asked. "Hey, did anyone check the attic? Because I mentioned that I'd seen a couple of old dog beds up there. I was going to bring one down for Cowboy to use in the main ranch house."

"Could he have gotten Cowboy up the attic stairs?" Rhetta asked doubtfully.

"Let's go check." And the two of them were off again, high energy.

Marnie snapped her fingers. "I'm going to organize folks to call everyone who left earlier. What if he slipped off with one of the other boys? I wouldn't put it past the little rascal to hide in the back of someone's van or truck."

As soon as Marnie left and they were alone, Lana turned to him. "Come on," she said, holding out a hand. "We're going to go search the cabin again."

"Good idea." They could see if Logan had taken food or supplies and get a read on the seriousness of his plan. At this point, Flint was hoping it *was* Logan's plan, not someone else's. There was that shady guy who'd tried to come into the pageant earlier. Flint doubled his pace, outdistancing Lana.

A quick check of the cabin and immediate surroundings revealed that indeed, he wasn't hiding anywhere.

They ran back up the stairs to search Logan's bedroom more carefully.

"People are fanning out now, checking a wider radius of the ranch," Lana reported, looking down at her rapidly pinging phone. "But I have a hunch we'll figure something out here."

Flint nodded, scanning the room. "His backpack. He usually hangs it up on that hook, but it's gone."

"Spider-Man, right? You check up here, I'll look downstairs."

Minutes later, having turned his room and Logan's inside out, he trotted down the stairs. "Find anything?"

She shook her head. "It doesn't look like

any food's missing, but I can't tell for sure. He could have grabbed some snacks."

"His favorite two shirts are missing. And his bear."

Lana gasped. "He planned this out."

Flint didn't want to think so, but all the evidence pointed in that direction.

"This is different from the other times he's run away, isn't it?"

"Yes, and I'm worried." Flint took one last look around the cabin and then opened the front door. "Come on, let's head for the main house. He's not here."

They walked quickly up the dirt road. Lana didn't say much, but she stayed right by his side, and Flint had the passing thought that there was no one else he'd rather have there.

All of a sudden he spotted something pale, right at the junction where the road to the ranch house diverged from the road leading to the ranch's exit. He hurried toward it, Lana right behind him.

There was Logan's bear, facedown on the

dusty road. A band seemed to clamp around Flint's chest, tighter and tighter.

"It's Buster!" Lana exclaimed, immediately recognizing the bear. "Oh, Flint, he must have come this way."

"Question is, where did he go from here?" Flint picked up the bear, brushed off the dirt and tucked it under his arm.

He looked up at the stars. *Keep him safe, Lord.*

And then, unable to stand still, he jumped the fence and started hunting the bushes, calling Logan's name.

"Flint. Flint!" Lana's voice pulled him back. "Stop a minute and let's think."

Flint did one last scan of the bushes and then climbed back over to where Lana stood.

She put a hand on his arm, steadying him. "Where could he be? Think. What's been going on with him?"

Flint drew in a breath and grabbed the fence post, impatient.

"There are lots of people searching. You know Logan best. Where could he be?"

Off at the ranch house and storage barn, he could hear people's voices, calling Logan's name and talking quietly. He *didn't* hear the excited sound he was hoping for, the sound of people finding Logan.

"What made him run away now, tonight?"

Flint mentally scanned the past couple of days. "He was upset about us fighting," he said. "About your leaving. Once that was said, he got quiet, and he hasn't been right since."

"Oh, Flint, I'm so sorry." Lana put a hand on his arm. "I just said that because I was hurt and embarrassed. I should have thought before I spoke."

Flint's heart leaped a little, and he squeezed her hand, taking in her flushed cheeks but not able to focus on the reason for them. "We came out of the barn, and he blurted out that question. About whether we were going to get married."

Lana's face went even pinker, but she nodded, going along with his reconstruction of the scene. "You said no, you weren't going to marry me."

There was something weird about the way she put it.

"And then," she continued, "I said I was leaving."

Flint snapped his fingers. "We've been talking about his mom some."

"Yeah?"

"Yeah. I paid attention to what you said, how it shouldn't be a big forbidden topic. I shouldn't have let him talk about her!"

Lana shook her head. "Talking with a loving parent *isn't* what causes problems for kids. What did he say?"

Flint took off his hat and ran a hand over his head. "He actually had a lot of misconceptions about it."

"Like what?"

"Like…" Flint frowned. "Like that it was his fault she left. He'd figured out that Stacie jumped ship right after he was born, so he'd been blaming himself." He shook his head. "I should've seen how much it was upsetting him."

"That's what kids do, Flint. They blame themselves. It's not your fault. If you think so, you're acting like a kid yourself."

That stopped him cold. She was right. "So if he blames himself for your leaving…" Flint was putting it together.

"Oh, Flint, how awful for him!" Lana's eyes filled with tears, shining dark in the moonlight. "Do you think that's how he interpretcd what happened?"

"Misinterpretation all around. But the question now is, what would he do next?"

She was tapping her thumb against her bottom lip. "We've been talking in Sunday school about taking your problems to God, and praying for forgiveness when you've been wrong. But he could have done that anywhere."

"Where do you pray in Sunday school?" Flint had a feeling they were onto something.

"We sit in a circle around the little altar we have in our classroom. But surely he wouldn't think of going so far as Haven, as the church?"

"Logan's used to running. He can get pretty far. And he's a determined kid." Flint jumped up and held out the stuffed bear. "Buster was right at the corner where he'd leave the ranch walking. Come on, I'm guessing he's walking to the church."

"Oh, no. It's so dark!" Lana's voice was choked. "And cars go so fast on that road. Should we walk or drive?"

"Drive. He could have been walking an hour, and that boy has some speed."

"I'm so glad he has Cowboy with him." Lana was already texting. "I'm telling everyone what we're doing."

"Come on, I'll get the truck."

"No." She tugged him toward the parking lot by the main ranch house. "Let's take my car."

"Why?" He started jogging toward the

barn where he'd left his truck. "I'll find him. I gotta find him."

Beside him, Lana grabbed his arm again and brought him to a halt. "*We'll* find him. We'll do it together. My car's low to the ground like Logan is. And Cowboy will respond to your call more than to mine." She frowned at him, every inch a severe teacher. "Don't be macho."

He blew out a breath. She was right. He squeezed her hand and turned with her to rush toward her car.

Logan was somewhere out there. "Let's go," he said, breaking into a run. "Every minute matters."

Lana climbed into the driver's seat of her subcompact as Flint squeezed into the passenger seat. She started the car and backed out, lowering all the windows as they cruised slowly along the road that led to the ranch gates.

Flint's fist clenched with what looked like impatience.

"What? Don't you think I should go slow?"

He blew out a sigh. "Yeah. I guess you're right. I just want to find him fast."

"And if we miss him the first time, it'll take twice as long."

"Right." He leaned out the window of the car as they turned out of the ranch and onto the highway. "Logan!"

Stars glittered overhead, and the moon peeked in and out of clouds. It was a beautiful night, a little chilly with a slight breeze that ruffled the bushes and trees.

Beautiful and terrifying, because a little boy was out here alone.

"Wait!" Flint was leaning out the window.

Lana slammed on the brake.

He opened the door and hurried to the ditch beside the road. Lana put the car in Park and got out, too, just in time to see Flint's shoulders slump. He was poking at the ditch with a stick. "It's just some old rags," he said.

The chorus of frogs, rising and falling, was a little eerie. A car careened by fast, its headlights flashing over them as the vehicle turned a curve and was gone.

Lana swallowed. To think of Logan being out here somewhere... She gripped Flint's hand as they turned back to the car. "I'm praying as hard as I can," she told him as she dropped his hand and hurried back to the driver's side.

As she drove slowly along, Flint leaned out the window. He alternated calling for Logan with whistling for Cowboy, and she could hear the stress and fear in his voice.

She ached for Flint. She ached for Logan. She loved both of them.

In this bigger framework, this real-world risk, Lana's own concerns shrank to their appropriate minor size. If Logan could be safe, the world would be good.

If they could all be together...well, that would be worth everything, and she'd never, ever take it for granted.

She heard a bark and slammed on the brakes again. "Could that be Cowboy?"

As they listened, the bark turned into a howl and then into a series of yips.

"That's not Cowboy," Flint said grimly. "That's coyotes."

"He has to be so scared!" As she put the car into gear to drive on, her hands slipped. She had to wipe them off on the sides of her jeans before she could hold on to the steering wheel.

They crept forward, now almost a mile from the ranch. "Wait." Flint gripped her arm. "Stop the car."

He whistled for Cowboy.

Out of the night came a black shape, running, hurling itself at the car.

Lana's heart thudded fast, and her throat went dry. But as the creature's claws clicked against the car door and she saw the familiar dark head and lolling tongue, she blew out a breath. "Cowboy!"

She pulled over carefully and turned off the car, and Flint got out and knelt in front of the dancing, tail-wagging dog. "Where's

Logan, boy?" He reached out to try to grab the dog, catching his collar.

At that, Cowboy barked frantically, and Flint let him go.

As soon as Cowboy was free of Flint's grip on his collar, he danced away, barking, seeming to gesture to them.

They jogged after the dog, Lana's heart pounding out of control.

And then she heard the sound of a little boy's cry, and Cowboy led them to a clump of tall grasses.

There, curled into a ball, crying, was Logan.

Lana gasped in a thankful breath. "Oh, Logan, we found you!"

"Are you hurt?" Flint demanded, scooping him up.

"Daddy!" Logan burrowed into Flint's arms. "I got scared!"

Lana fell to her knees and hugged Cowboy, who permitted a minute of attention and affection before bounding in circles around the three of them, barking, tail waving high.

"Come on," Flint said, his voice rough with emotion. "Let's get you home."

"Is he all right?" Lana hurried beside them, reaching out to touch Logan's blue-jeaned leg.

"I think he's going to be just fine."

Flint eased Logan into the small backseat. Lana popped open her trunk and found the fleece blanket she always carried there. She hurried forward and tucked it around Logan, just wanting to touch him herself, to feel that he was okay. Her eyes were damp with tears. "There you go. Nice and warm."

"Thanks, Miss Alvarez," he whispered, his voice sounding sleepy. "Daddy, can you sit back here with me?"

"Sure thing, buddy."

Lana climbed into the driver's seat and patted the passenger side for Cowboy, who jumped in, sitting tall. Lana texted Marnie, Rhetta and the rest, letting them know that Logan was safe, and they were on the way home.

* * *

After everyone had exclaimed over Logan, petted Cowboy, and hugged each other, the rest of the ranch staff and friends went home or into the main house. Flint had Logan in one arm, the blanket wrapped around him.

Lana was still on an adrenaline high, but she recognized that her role in this drama might be over. She didn't want it to be, but as Flint had said, she wasn't a part of the family. They'd go home, and she'd head for her lonely apartment. She stood, looking at the pair of them, and suddenly realized that Flint was reaching out a hand to her.

"Please," he said. "Come home with us for a little bit."

Her lips curved up into a smile. "You don't have to ask me twice."

Soon they were settled in the cabin's living room, with a sleepy Logan wrapped in a blanket in Flint's lap and Cowboy occupying the place of honor in front of the fire Flint had built.

"We'll talk more about this tomorrow, buddy," Flint said, "but can you tell me what made you run away?"

Logan squeezed Buster tighter. "I wanted to tell God I was sorry."

"About what?"

"About making Miss Alvarez go away and making you sad." He glanced from one to the other, his expression serious. "I know God answers our prayers. Only He wasn't answering when I prayed at home, so I thought maybe He would if I went to our special prayer place at church. But it was too far, and I was too scared, so I just prayed under the stars. Like you do, Daddy."

"And what did you pray for?" Flint asked.

"I want Miss Alvarez not to go away. I want her to stay and be my mom. But it's okay if it can't happen. God told me that when I was out in the night."

Lana blinked. "He told you?"

Logan nodded confidently. "He told me he would take care of me no matter what. But

I still got a little bit scared." He reached up and touched Lana's cheek. "And I still wish you could be my mom."

His simple assurance and clear expression of feelings made Lana's eyes well up. Oh, for the faith of a child.

Flint reached over and thumbed away the single tear that trickled down Lana's face. "I'm with Logan," he said softly. "I wish you'd stay."

"Stay in town?" Lana looked at him, her heart thumping a wild, erratic beat.

"Stay with *us*," he said. "I want you to stay with us."

Chapter Fourteen

An hour before the Christmas Eve service, Flint pulled into the church parking lot with Lana and Logan.

He felt indescribably blessed.

"Thanks for bringing us early," Lana said, smiling up at him as he opened the truck door for her. "I promised I'd help get the kids ready to sing. But Logan and I will come sit with you as soon as the kids' part is over."

"Sounds great." He squeezed her to his side as they hurried into the church. They'd spent most of the past few days together, hanging out at the cabin, doing chores on the ranch, baking cookies and watching Christmas movies.

Bonding like a family.

The church foyer was bright with evergreen boughs, red ribbons and two Christmas trees, all surrounding a large Nativity scene. From the sanctuary came the sounds of the adult choir practicing, their voices rising in beautiful Christmas music, cutting off and then repeating the same passage again, with laughter aplenty.

Lana immediately started shepherding kids to the classroom where they'd do a final rehearsal for their part of the musical service. Flint watched her bustling around and felt a satisfied smile curve his mouth. She was always going to be busy, helping out, organizing things, and he loved it. He just wanted to support her, so she didn't get burned out with all her caregiving.

He noticed that her purse was on the ground in front of the coatrack, standing open, so he picked it up and took it to the classroom. "I didn't want to dig into this," he said, "but it was open on the floor. You'd better make sure nobody's taken anything."

"Thanks." She gave him a quick, private smile and then took the purse and looked through it. "My wallet's here, and it doesn't look like anything's missing. Oh." She pulled out a white envelope. "Maybe this is what caused it to be moved."

"The mystery matchmakers." Flint chuckled. "Who's your beau supposed to be this time?"

"Open it!"

"Shh!"

Flint looked quickly at the kids in the room, but he couldn't tell which ones had spoken.

Lana ripped the note open and read it, holding it so he could see, as well.

Dear Miss Alvarez,
Please don't get married because last year a grate teacher, Miss Pringle, got

married to Mr. Hartwell and she moved away. The kids need you.

Lana grinned, grabbed a piece of wide-ruled paper and a marker, and penned a neat response. "Will you put this up on the bulletin board in the hall?" she asked Flint.

"Sure will." As he walked, he read it:

Dear Mystery Matchmakers: Please rest assured that no matter my marital status, I am committed to my job as a teacher at Haven Elementary School and at Haven Community Church.
Yours, Miss Alvarez.

Flint couldn't stop smiling as he pinned the note to the bulletin board.

The sound of angry boys' voices made him pause. Hearing the words "mystery matchmakers," he stepped back behind the coatrack, listening as the boys rushed into the sanctuary, arguing.

"You kids aren't the real mystery matchmakers! *We're* the mystery matchmakers, and we know what we're doing."

"We can do it, too! We wanted to keep Miss Alvarez here!'

"That's *not* what it's all about!"

Flint shook his head. Kids. It didn't seem like the matchmakers were doing any harm… and none of the voices he'd heard belonged to his son. So he'd let them have their squabbles.

He was turning toward the sanctuary, thinking to relax and listen to the various choirs practicing, when Gabe Everett gestured him over. He was standing with Heath and Tanner Barstow, the League's vice president.

"We have a problem," Gabe said quietly when Flint approached them. "You know how Pastor Andrew took up a special collection for the Boys Ranch last week?"

Flint nodded.

"It's missing." Quickly, Gabe filled him in: the collection had been in a drawer in the church office. Now it was missing, and the lock had been tampered with. "There's been dozens of people in and out of here in the past week, but we're suspecting it's the saboteur who's been targeting the Boys Ranch."

"Could be anyone."

"There was other money around the office that wasn't taken. Just the envelope marked 'Boys Ranch.'"

Flint crossed his arms. "Fletcher's against the ranch, but I can't figure him for stealing money from a bunch of kids."

"Avery's a different story," Tanner said.

Flint shook his head. "Shame that someone would do that, at Christmas, in our little town."

"Just keep your eyes and ears open," Heath said to Flint. "We all are." He raised a hand to someone across the room, then headed over to stand by Josie.

"Any word on your grandfather?" Flint asked Gabe.

Gabe shook his head. "Still working on it."

So it was Christmas, and things were good. Not perfect; there were a few problems that still needed fixing here in Haven. But for now, he was going into church to meditate on all that was going right. And to give thanks to the Creator who'd made it so.

After the children had performed, Lana walked out into the sanctuary to sit by Flint and Logan. She felt a little self-conscious, doing that in front of everyone in town, but she also felt secure in their relationship. Especially when Flint put an arm around her. She spent the rest of the service in a daze of love and happiness, celebrating and thanking God for the many gifts he'd given her.

Even in this early service, they lit the candles, one person to another. Inhaling the scent of bayberry and pine, helping Logan light his candle, Lana caught Flint's eyes on her and blushed.

After the service, as they headed through the crowds toward the peppermint cocoa that was a Christmas Eve tradition in Haven, Marnie Binder came bustling up. "Look what someone handed me," she said, beaming. "It's for you."

Lana took the small jewelry-sized box, clumsily wrapped, and read the tag on it. "From Flint," it said.

She looked over at where Flint was talking to a couple of his League friends. She held up the box, pointed at it.

He shrugged and raised his hands.

Of course, it wasn't really from him. She pocketed it to open later.

Across the foyer, she noticed Avery Culpepper. So the woman had come to church again. And Lana was pleased to notice that she didn't feel any more anger toward the woman. With God's help, she'd been able to forgive. That was good.

Then she realized that Avery was hanging on to the arm of Eduardo Gomez. She frowned, disconcerted, as Katie came up beside her. "Do you think they're an item?" she asked.

"Doesn't look like it." Katie nodded at them, and Lana saw Eduardo gently disengage himself from Avery's clutches and head over to talk to a pretty, dark-haired woman whose daughter was playing with Eduardo's daughter, Valentina. "Looks like Eduardo has other ideas."

Lana smiled but turned away, not wanting to seem like a gossip. "You look pretty," she said, noticing Katie's black-and-red dress and heels.

"It's not like anyone will notice," Katie said glumly.

"Don't give up!" Lana wanted everyone in the world to feel the same peaceful sense of love that she was feeling.

As they walked toward the refreshment table, Pastor Andrew came out of his office. When he saw Katie, he dropped the stack of programs he'd been carrying.

Katie hurried to help him, and as they

smiled at each other, Lana hoped that meant they'd at least develop a friendship.

Just then, Logan and two of his boys ranch friends ran out of the classroom area...directly toward Fletcher Snowden Phillips and several of his friends, all well up in years.

Lana gasped and started forward. The last thing they needed was another disaster here at the church, someone else knocked down.

But Logan glanced up, noticed Fletcher and his friends, and slowed down, yelling "careful!" to the two other boys. They stopped, too, and the trio walked sedately past the elders.

Fletcher reached down and ruffled Logan's hair.

"It's a Christmas wish come true," Flint said behind her, a smile in his voice.

She leaned back against him, savoring his warmth. "It sure is."

Then, not wanting to make a spectacle of their budding relationship, she pulled away, took a step to create a respectable distance between them, and turned toward Flint. As various conversations buzzed around them, she pulled out the little jewelry box. "I got a gift from you," she teased, showing him the handwritten note attached to the box.

He raised an eyebrow. "Better open it."

When she did, there was a bubblegum-machine ring inside, along with another note. "Will you marry me and stay in Haven forever?"

She giggled, feeling her face heat. She and Flint had talked a lot about the future in the past few days, but there'd been no formal engagement.

"That reminds me," Flint said. "I got you a real Christmas present." He reached into his pocket and pulled out a small box, wrapped in silver paper.

She took it, eyes wide, heart pounding.

He got you jewelry. That's nice and romantic. You can't expect anything more.

But as Flint sank to one knee, smiling up at her, she felt the reality of God's promise rushing in. *Exceedingly abundantly above all that we ask or think.*

Around them, the church had gotten quiet. People were watching, not even pretending to mind their own business.

Flint gestured to Logan, who raced over, grinning. Apparently, this move had been planned between the two of them. "Lana, I love you," Flint said, loud and clear. "Will you marry me, be my wife?" He was a man of few words, but the tenderness on his face and in his eyes said it all.

Logan knelt beside his father. "And will you be my mom?"

A collective "awwwwww" swept around the room.

Through tears, Lana saw so many happy, expectant faces around her: Katie, Rhetta, Bea, Marnie, the boys from the ranch and all the staff.

And before her, the man—and the boy—whom she loved with all her heart. She bent down and pulled them up, and Flint's arms came around both her and Logan. "I would love to be your wife and mother," she whispered just for them to hear.

"She said yes!" Logan shouted.

And amid the laughter and hugs, the congratulations and happy tears, Lana spared a glance upward to the author of it all, the Creator who had turned three people's sadness into joy.

Abundant blessings. For her, for Flint and Logan, for all of them.

She closed her eyes in praise.

* * * * *

If you liked this
LONE STAR COWBOY LEAGUE:
BOYS RANCH *novel,*
watch for the next book,
THE COWBOY'S TEXAS FAMILY by
Margaret Daley, available January 2017.

And don't miss a single story in the
LONE STAR COWBOY LEAGUE:
BOYS RANCH *miniseries:*

Book #1:
THE RANCHER'S TEXAS MATCH
by Brenda Minton

Book #2:
THE RANGER'S TEXAS PROPOSAL
by Jessica Keller

Can't get enough
LONE STAR COWBOY LEAGUE?
Check out the original
LONE STAR COWBOY LEAGUE
miniseries from Love Inspired,
starting with
A REUNION FOR THE RANCHER
by Brenda Minton.

And travel back in time with
LONE STAR COWBOY LEAGUE:
THE FOUNDING YEARS,
a Love Inspired Historical miniseries,
starting with
STAND-IN RANCHER DADDY
by Renee Ryan.

Both titles and full miniseries
available now!

Find more great reads at
www.LoveInspired.com

Dear Reader,

I hope you enjoyed your latest visit to Haven, Texas, as much as I did! Flint and Lana are close to my heart because they've both suffered in the past, and both are tempted to close themselves off to love, so they won't be hurt again. But God—with an assist from Marnie Binder and Logan—has other plans. As so often happens, though, it's up to Flint and Lana to take a leap of faith and trust that God has good plans for them. In fact, God's plans are exceedingly abundant, beyond anything we could dream up ourselves. That's a truth we should all embrace and celebrate during this Christmas season!

If you'd like to learn about my new releases and get a free romance story, please hop over to my website at http://www.leetobinmcclain. com and sign up for my newsletter. Or send me an email via the website. I love to hear from readers!

Wishing you abundant blessings,
Lee